MEL⊙DY
1964
No Ordinary Sound

By Denise Lewis Patrick

★ American Girl®

Melody's Family
and Friends

Yvonne, Lila, and Dwayne
Melody's sisters
and brother

Daddy and Mommy
Melody's parents

Big Momma
Melody's
grandmother

Poppa
Melody's
grandfather

Tish and Charles
Val's parents. Charles is Mommy's cousin

Val
Melody's favorite cousin

Sharon
Melody's best friend

Bo
The family dog

Miss Esther
A neighbor and member of Melody's church

Miss Dorothy
The children's choir director at church and Big Momma's best friend

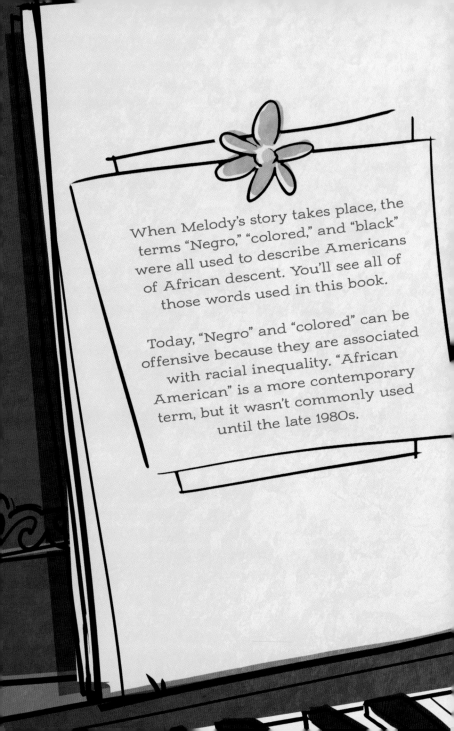

When Melody's story takes place, the terms "Negro," "colored," and "black" were all used to describe Americans of African descent. You'll see all of those words used in this book.

Today, "Negro" and "colored" can be offensive because they are associated with racial inequality. "African American" is a more contemporary term, but it wasn't commonly used until the late 1980s.

Table of Contents

Meet the Ellisons

♪ CHAPTER 1 ♪

It was a perfect day in May, and Melody Ellison could hardly wait for her father to pull the car to a stop in front of her grandparents' house. Every Sunday, Melody and her family had dinner here after church. But today was different. Melody was almost bursting with news. She hopped out of the station wagon so quickly that she forgot to hold the door for her sister Lila, who was coming out behind her.

"Hey!" Lila shouted, but nine-year-old Melody was already on the front porch, peering into the front windows. She could hear music coming from inside, and couldn't help tapping her shiny shoes. Music always made her want to *move*.

"What are you so hot after?" asked Dwayne, Melody's older brother. His long legs had brought him around the car and up behind her in only a few steps.

"I'm not hot," Melody answered, before she realized that Dwayne was joking. He meant that she was excited, and she was. She couldn't hold in her news any longer.

"Miss Dorothy asked me to sing a solo for Youth Day,"

she said proudly. Youth Day was far away in October, but it was the biggest children's program at their church. Kids from all over the city came to sing, play music, recite poetry, and even perform in skits. Only a few kids got the chance to stand in front to sing solo parts, and they had to be very, very good.

Dwayne raised his eyebrows, and Melody watched his face nervously. It wasn't easy to impress him. Dwayne was eighteen, and he'd done his first solo when he was eight.

"Wow, congratulations!" he said. "You've gotta write Yvonne and tell her."

Melody grinned. Yvonne was their oldest sister, who was away at college. She was a good singer, too. In fact, all the members of Melody's family were musical. "I will," she promised. "As soon as we get home."

"Tell Yvonne what?" Lila joined them, carrying a plate with their mother's foil-wrapped triple-chocolate cake.

"Melody's going to be the star of the New Hope Baptist Church Youth Day," Dwayne said, grabbing the plate as it wobbled. "Just like I'm going to be the biggest Motown star since Smokey Robinson."

Lila sniffed matter-of-factly. "Dee-Dee might beat you to it." Lila was thirteen and sometimes acted like she knew everything in the world.

"Not me." Melody shook her head. She liked to pretend

she was a singing star at home, using her hairbrush as a microphone. But she didn't like to be in the spotlight. She felt safe in the children's choir when the congregation was full of the church family she'd known all her life. But she was nervous about standing alone on Youth Day, in front of a big crowd full of faces she didn't know.

Melody's parents crowded onto the porch as Big Momma swung open the door. Melody had always thought it was funny that they called her grandmother Big Momma, since she wasn't especially tall. But the name was a sign of respect. Besides, when her grandmother sang, her voice was very big.

"Hello, my chicks!" Big Momma said, waving everyone inside. She greeted each of her grandchildren with a rose-scented squeeze.

"Big Momma, this is Detroit, Michigan. You left all your chickens back in Alabama, remember?" Dwayne said, ducking out of her arms.

After giving Melody a hug, Big Momma folded her arms and gave her a stern look. "I believe you've got something to tell me," she said.

"Yes!" Melody exclaimed. "Miss Dorothy asked me to learn a solo over the summer for the Youth Day pro—" She stopped. Big Momma was smiling and nodding. "You already knew!" Melody said. "How?"

"Big Momma and Miss Dorothy are best friends," Lila said. "They tell each other everything."

Big Momma laughed. "Yes, Dorothy and I trained to be music teachers together back in Alabama. She says you're ready to carry a song on your own."

"Who is ready for what?" Melody's mother asked from the dining room.

"Melody's doing a Youth Day solo," Lila told her.

"Oh, that's wonderful, honey!" Mrs. Ellison clapped her hands and rushed to give Melody a hug.

"I believe our Melody is ready to sing out," Mr. Ellison said as he placed extra chairs at the dining table. Melody heard the pride in her father's voice and wished she felt as confident as he did.

Big Momma put her arm around Melody's shoulders. "It's okay to be nervous, baby chick," she said, reading Melody's mind. "You have all summer to practice. I'll help."

"But what about your students?" Melody asked. Big Momma taught piano and voice lessons to kids and grown-ups, right in her living room.

"Don't worry, I'll find the time."

"Thanks, Big Momma." Melody felt her nerves flutter again. But she felt good knowing that her family believed in her so much. She skipped into the dining room to join Lila, Dwayne, and their parents at the table.

Melody sat next to Mommy and looked at Dwayne, who was at the other end of the table. "The thing about Youth Day is that I get to pick my own song," Melody told her brother. "But I don't know which one to sing."

"We could try some songs after dinner." Dwayne winked at Melody. She knew he took every chance he could to play Big Momma's beloved piano.

"*After* dinner means we need to *eat* dinner first, doesn't it?" Melody's father said.

"But we can't start without Poppa," Dwayne said.

Where was her grandfather, anyway, Melody wondered. Before she could ask, she heard the back door of the house open and shut.

"Hello!" Poppa's voice boomed. Poppa always talked loud. Melody's mother said it was because of his work around all the loud machines years ago at the auto factory. Melody liked the sound—it reminded her of drumbeats.

"Guess who I brought to dinner!" Poppa called from the kitchen.

Everyone turned in his direction. He opened the door, and there stood Yvonne with a huge smile on her face.

"Vonnie!" Melody ran around the table to give her big sister a hug.

"What a surprise!" Mrs. Ellison said. "We didn't expect you till next week." Melody could tell that her mother was very happy. Yvonne had been gone since January.

"I took all my exams and I finished my last paper early, so I caught the bus," Yvonne explained. "Poppa picked me up at the Detroit terminal. Boy, that ride from Alabama takes forever!" She barely took a breath before dropping her bag and greeting everyone. "Wow, Dee-Dee. Did you get taller? Got any new sounds, Dwayne? Lila, are those new glasses? Dad, you're wearing the birthday shirt we gave you! Big Momma, that roast smells really good. And Mommy, I know you made your triple-chocolate cake. Can we eat?"

Melody laughed. College hadn't changed Yvonne's habit of talking a mile a minute.

Big Momma brought the roast in and everyone took their places around the table, with Poppa at one end and Daddy at the other. And now the family was truly all together, the way their Sundays used to be.

"Dee-Dee, why don't you sing grace for us?" her father said.

"Yes, Daddy," Melody said. She felt comfortable singing in front of *this* crowd. She bowed her head and sang in a strong, clear voice:

> *By Thy hands must we be fed;*
> *Give us, Lord, our daily bread.*

Table Talk

♫ **CHAPTER 2** ♫

So," Yvonne said, "what's the news? What have I been missing?" She glanced around the table.

"I'm doing double shifts at the factory again this week," Daddy told her.

"There's a lot of talk about some of the city schools only having half days next year," Mommy said.

Everyone looked up at that. "Really?" Yvonne asked.

Mommy nodded. "Can you believe that? School for just three hours a day? We teachers are against it, but the district says there may not be enough money for full days."

"I have news . . ." Melody started to say. But Yvonne nodded in Dwayne's direction.

"What's up with you?" she asked him.

"Not much," Dwayne said, leaning over his almost empty plate.

Melody looked at him curiously. When he wasn't working at the factory, Dwayne was always busy singing with his friends or writing new music. Why would he tell Yvonne "not much"? She wanted to ask him, but she also wanted her turn to share her news.

"Vonnie," Melody said. "I was going to write you, but now I can tell you in person."

"Spill it, Dee-Dee!" Yvonne laughed.

"I'm going to sing my first solo!"

"In the Mother's Day program next week?" Yvonne asked.

"No, Miss Dorothy picked me for the Youth Day program. I have the whole summer to learn a song."

"That's great!" Yvonne said. "Now you can show that girl—what's her name? The one who always tries to boss the other singers around?"

"You mean Diane Harris?" Melody made a face. Diane was in the same fourth-grade class as Melody and took piano lessons from Big Momma. She had a nice voice, but she wasn't at all nice about that.

"I hear she's a solo hog," Dwayne mumbled with his mouth full.

"We can't be jealous of other people's gifts," Mommy said to Dwayne sternly. She turned to Melody. "Besides, didn't you just say that Miss Dorothy asked *you* to sing a solo?"

"Yes." Melody looked down, twiddling her fingers in her lap. "But I'm really not as good as Diane."

"Who says that?" Daddy asked.

Melody said out loud what she'd been thinking since

Miss Dorothy's request. "Well, Diane has a big, grown-up voice, and I only have a girl voice."

"Everybody's got a right to shine, baby chick," Big Momma said. "Diane does and you do, too. You've got a beautiful voice."

Melody couldn't help but worry. She remembered music easily, but she had to practice to get the words right. Diane was so sure of herself when she sang! She could hear a song once and sing it without one mistake.

"You'll make it work, Melody," Mommy said. "I know you'll give it your best effort." Mommy turned to Yvonne. "Speaking of effort, how was your second year at Tuskegee?"

"Did you study all the time, Vonnie?" Melody asked. Mommy had gone to Tuskegee University in Alabama, and this year Dwayne had applied and been accepted.

Yvonne shook her head so that her small earrings sparkled. "There's so much more to do at school besides studying," she said, reaching for more gravy.

"Like what?" Poppa asked, propping his elbows on the table.

"Well, last week before finals a bunch of us went out to help black people in the community register to vote," Yvonne said. "And do you know, a lady told me she was too afraid to sign up."

"Why was she afraid?" Melody interrupted.

"Because somebody threw a rock through her next-door neighbor's window after her neighbor voted," Yvonne explained, her eyes flashing with anger. "This is 1963! How can anybody get away with that?"

Melody looked from Yvonne to her father. "You always say not voting is like not being able to talk. Why would anyone not want to talk?"

Daddy sighed. "It's not that she doesn't want to vote, Melody. There are a lot of unfair rules down South that keep our people from exercising their rights. Some white people will do anything, including scaring black people, to keep change from happening. They don't want to share jobs or neighborhoods or schools with us. Voting is like a man's or woman's voice speaking out to change those laws and rules."

"And it's not just about voting," Mommy said. "Remember what Rosa Parks did in Montgomery? She stood up for her rights."

"You mean she *sat down* for her rights," Melody said. Melody knew all about Mrs. Parks, who got arrested for simply sitting down on a city bus. She had paid her fare like everybody else, but because she was a Negro the bus driver told her she had to give her seat to a white person! *But that happened eight years ago,* Melody realized. *Why haven't things changed?*

"Aren't we just as good as anybody else?" Melody asked as she looked around the table. "The laws should be fair everywhere, for everybody, right?"

"That's not always the way life works," Poppa said.

"Why not?" Lila asked.

Poppa sat back and rubbed his silvery mustache. That always meant he was about to tell a story.

"Back in Alabama, there was a white farmer who owned the land next to ours. Palmer was his name. Decent fellow. We went into town the same day to sell our peanut crops. It wasn't a good growing year, but I'd lucked out with twice as many sacks of peanuts as Palmer. Well, at the market they counted and weighed his sacks. Then they counted and weighed my sacks. Somehow Palmer got twice as much money as I got for selling half the crop I had. They never even checked the quality of what we had, either."

"What?" Lila blurted out.

"How?" Melody scooted to the edge of her chair. She'd never seen the old family farm, so she was always interested in stories about it.

"Wait, now." Poppa waved his grandchildren quiet. "I asked the man to weigh the peanuts again, but he refused. I complained. Even Palmer spoke up for me. But that man turned to me and said, 'Boy—'"

"He called you *boy*?" Dwayne interrupted, putting his fork down.

"'Boy,'" Poppa continued, "'this is all you're gonna get. And if you keep up this trouble, you won't have any farm to go back to!'"

Melody's mouth fell open. "What was he talking about? You did have a farm," she said, glancing at Big Momma.

"He meant we were in danger of losing our farm—our home—because your grandfather spoke out to a white man," Big Momma explained. She shook her head slowly. "As hard as we'd worked to buy that land, as hard as it was for colored people to own anything in Alabama, we decided that day that we had to sell and move north."

Melody sighed. Maybe the lady Yvonne mentioned didn't want to risk losing *her* home if she "spoke out" by voting. But Yvonne was right—it was hard to understand how that could happen in the United States of America in 1963!

Poppa was shaking his head. "It's a shame that colored people today still have to be afraid of standing up or speaking out for themselves."

"Negroes," Mommy corrected him.

"Black people," Yvonne said firmly.

"What *are* we supposed to call ourselves?" Lila asked.

Melody thought about how her grandparents usually said "colored." They were older and from the South, and

Big Momma said that's what was proper when they were growing up. Mommy and Daddy mostly said "Negroes." But ever since she went to college, Yvonne was saying "black people." Melody noticed that Mommy and Daddy were saying it sometimes, too. Melody spoke up. "What about 'Americans'?" she suggested.

Yvonne still seemed upset. "That's right, Dee-Dee. We're Americans. We have the same rights as white Americans. There shouldn't be any separate water fountains or waiting rooms or public bathrooms. Black

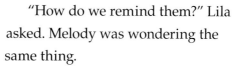

Americans deserve equal treatment and equal pay. And sometimes we have to remind people."

"How do we remind them?" Lila asked. Melody was wondering the same thing.

"By not shopping at stores that won't hire black workers," Yvonne explained. "By picketing in front of a restaurant that won't serve black people. By marching."

"You won't catch me protesting or picketing or marching in any street," Dwayne announced, working on his third helping of potatoes. "I'm gonna be onstage or in the recording studio, making music and getting famous."

Daddy shook his head, and Melody knew there was

going to be another argument, the way there always was when Dwayne talked about becoming a music star.

"Don't forget," Daddy said, "when you graduated high school early, we agreed that you'd work in the factory until the summer was over, and then go on to college. I couldn't go to college, and now I'm working double shifts at a factory so you can! You could *study* music in college!"

Mommy was nodding. Melody knew that her parents were disappointed whenever Dwayne talked about skipping college. She saw Dwayne stop eating to look down at his plate and she felt bad for her brother. Melody hated when he and Daddy argued. So when Dwayne looked as if he might say something, Melody interrupted.

"Daddy," Melody said. "Dwayne can sing and write music already, and he can play the piano almost as good as Big Momma can. He's really talented. It's like Big Momma says—everybody's got a right to shine."

Daddy looked at Melody. "But with a college degree, your brother would have a whole lot of opportunities."

"Let's save this talk for later," Mommy said.

Melody blew out a relieved breath. She didn't want their great day to be ruined by a disagreement.

"I say everybody needs some cake," Big Momma said. She got up and headed for the kitchen.

While Mommy and Lila began to clear the dishes,

Dwayne escaped to the living room. Yvonne stayed at the table, talking to their father and grandfather about her plans for a summer job. Melody wandered to the archway between the rooms. Dwayne was playing Big Momma's piano, making up a new song. Melody listened for him to sing some words, but there weren't any. Maybe he hadn't thought of them yet.

The phone beside the sofa rang. "Children, answer that for me!" Big Momma called from the kitchen.

Melody started into the living room, but Dwayne had already grabbed the telephone receiver.

"Hello!" Dwayne answered breathlessly. And then, instead of calling either of his grandparents or taking a message, he lowered his voice.

"Yeah?" he almost whispered. "Make it quick. I told you this is my grandfather's number. Okay. I'm working on the song now. I'll meet you later."

"Who is it?" Poppa asked from the table. Dwayne dropped the receiver into the cradle with a clatter.

"Are you getting calls from your girlfriends on my telephone?" Poppa laughed. So did Daddy and Yvonne.

"No, sir," Dwayne called quickly. His eyes met Melody's. He had a funny expression on his face. Dwayne definitely had a secret.

"Was that about your singing group?" Melody asked.

Dwayne pulled her farther into the living room. "Yeah, but after that scrape with Dad, I'd rather not announce this, okay? That was Artie's brother. He just got hired as a musician at Motown, and he's gonna try to get us an audition." Artie was Dwayne's buddy and a member of his singing group, The Detroiters.

"That's so exciting, Dwayne!" Melody exclaimed.

"Shhh," Dwayne insisted. "Can you keep it a secret?"

Melody pinched her finger and thumb together and slid them across her lips as if she were closing a zipper. That was the signal she and her brother and sisters used with one another, meaning, "I won't tell anyone!"

Dwayne's shoulders relaxed, and he went back to the piano. Melody followed.

Dwayne held his hands dramatically over the piano keys. "How about you singing this for your Youth Day solo?" he said, beginning to play and sing something different—and lively. *"Grandpa Poppa had a farm . . ."*

Melody giggled, shaking her head at how he'd changed the words of the old kindergarten rhyme. From all around the house, her family joined in:

"E-i-e-i-ohhhh!"

Let Your Light Shine

♫ CHAPTER 3 ♫

Melody didn't say a word about Dwayne's secret to her sisters. But the tune that he had been playing on Big Momma's piano snuck into Melody's head the next morning and stayed there all day long. By the time she was walking home from school with her best friend, Sharon, Melody was humming her brother's nameless, wordless tune out loud.

"What's that song?" Sharon asked. "Is it something you're going to sing for Youth Day?"

"Just music in my head," Melody said. She wouldn't give away Dwayne's new creation, even to Sharon.

"Well, what *are* you going to sing?" Sharon asked as they approached her house.

"I don't know yet," Melody answered. "But Big Momma and Dwayne both promised to help me."

Sharon stopped at her front gate and grinned. "Well, then, you're going to be great whatever you choose. See you at choir rehearsal," she called as she opened the gate and hurried up the walk.

Melody walked three blocks to her own house. She

hoped that Yvonne was home and that she and Lila and Melody could spend time together the way they used to before Yvonne went away to college. They ate cookies and combed one another's hair and talked about anything that popped into their heads. The "sister-thing" was what Yvonne called it.

When Melody opened the front door, Bo, their small terrier, ran to her, barking excitedly. Melody bent to pet him, and Bo rolled onto his back and stuck his paws in the air.

Lila was already home from junior high, and she was sitting at the dining room table, doing homework. Melody looked at the stack of mail on the table. There was a small purple envelope with her name written in careful cursive handwriting. "I got a letter from Val," Melody said. Val was their cousin who lived in Alabama, and she was between Lila and Melody in age. Val and Melody had been pen pals since Melody was in second grade. Melody opened the envelope and began reading out loud.

"You'll explode when you hear my news. We are moving to Detroit as soon as school is over! What?" Melody screamed. This news was even more surprising than Dwayne's secret.

Even Lila was surprised. "That's big!" she said.

"What's big?" Yvonne yawned, padding downstairs barefoot and still in pajamas.

Melody waved the letter in the air. "Val and her mom and dad are moving to Detroit!"

"That sure is news," Yvonne said. "I wonder what made Charles and Tish decide to move?"

"I don't know," Melody answered. "But I can't wait!"

"This calls for a celebration, don't you think?" Yvonne asked.

"Yes!" Both Lila and Melody answered at once.

"Great." Yvonne rubbed her hands together. "We should start by raiding Dwayne's cookie stash."

Lila grinned. "They're hidden in the cupboard—"

"—behind the tuna fish!" Melody finished.

When Dwayne came home from his factory job an hour later, the house was full of loud singing coming from upstairs. There was an empty vanilla wafer box on the kitchen table.

"This little light of mine, I'm gonna let it shine!"

"Oh, man! Not the sister-thing again!" Dwayne yelled. But no one heard him over the laughter, which was even louder than the singing.

♫

That evening, after a quick dinner, Melody's mother drove the girls to choir rehearsal. Yvonne decided to tag along. Melody had been so busy getting her homework done that she hadn't had a chance to tell her mother about Val's move until they were all in the car. Her mother didn't seem surprised.

"Big Momma told me a few weeks ago," Mommy said. "Until they find a house of their own, they'll be staying with Big Momma and Poppa."

Melody's grandparents lived a few blocks away from the Ellisons. "That means I can walk over to see Val all the time," Melody said. "We can do everything together!"

"Val has lived in Birmingham her whole life," Lila told Melody matter-of-factly. "Detroit sure is different. It's going to take her a while to get used to things."

"Do you think Val is bringing her bike?" Melody asked.

Mommy shook her head. "Most of their things will be in storage. You girls will have to share some of your things with Val. You'll have to—"

"Make it work," both Mommy and Melody said at the same time. Melody sounded exactly like Mommy, which made everyone laugh as they pulled up in front of New Hope Baptist Church.

When Melody got out of the car, she heard the voices of the adult choir floating out of the open doors. She ran up the steps into the church and sat on the first pew inside the door. She closed her eyes and soaked in the sounds.

"This is my story, this is my song." A single soprano voice sang the words clearly. The music echoed inside Melody's body. She opened her eyes and looked at the tall stained-glass windows. On Sunday mornings, they sparkled like jewels when the sunshine poured in.

Melody's sisters slid onto the bench, one on either side, and she was squeezed between them just like when she was small and Yvonne snuck her lemon drops to keep her from wiggling during the service. Melody smiled to herself at the memory. Now that she was older, she didn't wiggle during church. She listened to the pastor and to the music. She loved the Sundays when the children's choir sang and she stood in front, looking out at her family. Melody also loved the Sundays when she sat in the pews with her whole family. It was one of the few times they were all together. *And soon Val will be here, too!* she thought.

Melody listened to the last lines of the hymn.

> *Watching and waiting, looking above,*
> *Filled with His goodness, lost in His love.*

That's how Melody felt in church. There was goodness all around. When the song ended, it seemed that her heart beat a little bit differently.

Melody was still swaying to the tune inside her head

when Miss Dorothy walked past, shuffling her sheet music.

"Let's go." Lila pulled Melody up as the adults filed out of the choir stand. Melody saw Sharon come in, and she watched Diane take her seat in the front row.

As everyone gathered, Miss Dorothy started playing the piano softly. She knew everything about music. Like Big Momma, Miss Dorothy could read and play from sheet music, or she could hear a tune and then play it without any music at all.

When all the children were in place, Miss Dorothy walked in front of the choir and stood with her hands clasped behind her back. That was the sign for everyone to stop talking.

"All right, choir," she said. "This Sunday is Mother's Day, and we'll be honoring all the New Hope mothers. We want to do our very best, don't we?"

"Yes, Miss Dorothy!"

"Remember that this will be our last choir rehearsal for this school year," Miss Dorothy went on. "I know all of you will spend some time singing over the summer. When school begins in September, we'll begin practicing for Youth Day. Melody, our soloist—I want you to find a song to sing. Your grandmother and I will start working on it with you over the summer if you'd like."

"Yes, Miss Dorothy," Melody said happily.

Diane leaned over to the girl next to her and loudly whispered, "If *I* were doing a solo, I wouldn't need the whole summer to practice."

Melody felt her face burn with hot embarrassment. Yvonne, who was sitting in the back of the church, stood up and crossed her arms over her chest. Melody was afraid she might say something, but then Miss Dorothy cleared her throat. Yvonne sat down again.

"Remember, even when one of us does a solo, we all work together," Miss Dorothy said sternly. "We all support one another. That's very important in a choir. The chorus helps the soloist. The soloist helps the chorus." She clicked her baton on the edge of the piano. "Now, choir, rise!"

Everyone stood. After Miss Dorothy led the group in vocal warm-ups, she repositioned the microphone in front of Diane, who was doing a solo for Mother's Day.

Diane stood straight and tall. She didn't blink. She didn't seem nervous at all. Melody had to admit that when she thought of her own faraway solo, she thought about what could go wrong. When Diane sang by herself, she acted as if she expected that everything would go right.

Miss Dorothy played the first chords of "His Eye Is on the Sparrow." Diane began to sing, and she did sound wonderful. When it was time for the chorus, Melody sang out with all her heart.

I sing because I'm happy. I sing because I'm free.
His eye is on the sparrow, and I know He watches me.

Melody felt the entire choir's sound swell around her, and she was filled with a peaceful calm that made her feel happy and free.

♪

The next day, Melody went to Big Momma's house after school. She wanted to make a "Welcome" sign for Val. Big Momma kept a shoe box full of art supplies. She called it the "just in case" box, just in case somebody wanted to create something beautiful.

Melody found the box and some construction paper and set everything on the table in the dining room as Big Momma came downstairs.

"I think we should have a welcome party for Val and her parents," Melody told her grandmother excitedly. "I'm going to make a banner."

Big Momma smiled in approval. "That sounds like a fine idea," she said. "You go on and work quietly in the kitchen, though. It's time for my first afternoon lesson."

Melody gathered her supplies and went to the kitchen, closing the door behind her as the doorbell rang. As she began to outline the word "WELCOME" in big block

Melody felt the entire choir's sound swell around her, and she was filled with a peaceful calm that made her feel happy and free.

letters, she heard the low hum of Big Momma's voice, a few piano chords, and then a familiar child's voice.

It was Diane Harris! Melody stopped working to listen.

Diane's fingers fumbled over the piano keys. "Try again," Big Momma said calmly.

The choppy playing started and stopped, and then started over very slowly.

"Go on, go on." Big Momma sounded encouraging. But suddenly the piano was silent.

"Mrs. Porter, I can't do it!" Diane said. "I'll never play the piano as well as I can sing."

What had happened to Diane's sure and steady choir voice? Melody wondered. Diane sounded just the way Melody felt about doing a solo—nervous.

"This is new for you," Big Momma said to Diane. "Don't be afraid of what you don't know."

Melody felt that Big Momma was speaking directly to her about the Youth Day solo.

Big Momma went on. "You have to take your time and open your heart to learning. You can shine with this instrument if you work hard enough."

In the kitchen, Melody smiled. *Maybe Diane and I are more alike than we are different.* Melody picked up her crayon again, and drew a big yellow sun in the corner of her sign.

Dances and Dollars

♫ CHAPTER 4 ♫

On Thursday afternoon, Poppa picked Melody up from school so that she could help him in his flower shop. Poppa knew all about growing things. Back in Alabama he had grown vegetables and fruit trees as well as peanuts on his farm, and he had an enormous flower garden. He'd taught Melody how to plan a garden and how to care for it through all the different seasons. When her flowers bloomed, Melody loved to pick a bouquet and arrange it so that all the blossoms looked their best. Putting different colors and shapes together reminded her of different voices blending together in the choir. Melody had learned so much that now Poppa let her work in the shop sorting his weekly flower shipment and getting ready for the big weekend orders.

Melody settled back in the worn seat of his old work truck. It smelled like warm soil and flower petals. She inhaled deeply.

"How was school today?" Poppa asked, shifting gears.

"It was okay," Melody said, looking out her window.

"Just okay? Hmm. Well, I have an idea that I think is

more than okay." Poppa slowed on 12th Street in front of
his shop, Frank's Flowers, and pulled the truck around to
the delivery entrance at the back. "How would you like
to make a special arrangement for your mother and Big
Momma for Mother's Day?"

"Yes!" Melody said, jumping out of the truck.

They stepped into the workroom, which was one
of Melody's favorite places. An old wooden worktable
stretched along the length of one wall, and shelves held
vases of every shape and size, rolls of ribbon, floral tape,
pins, and other supplies. There was always music on the
radio. This afternoon it was jazz.

Melody dropped her book bag beside the door. There
was a long cardboard box at one end of the table.

"Go on, look," Poppa said.

Melody lifted the top of the box with both hands.
"Ohhh!" she gasped. The box wasn't full of candy, or toys,
or anything else that would delight most nine-year-olds.
The box was filled with red roses, pink freesia, and feath-
ery green ferns.

Melody looked up at Poppa. "Can I really make this one
all by myself?"

"Yes, you can, Little One," Poppa said, taking a delicate
china vase from the shelf. "When you're done, we'll leave it
here in the cooler so it stays fresh. I'll bring it to the house

early Sunday morning, and I'll hide it so your grandmother doesn't see it until after church. Watch out for the thorns."

"I will!" Melody said. She opened a drawer and took out the girl-size gardening gloves that she kept at the store. She pulled on the gloves and carefully picked up one of the roses. She was so busy imagining how she would mix the colors and flowers in the vase that she didn't notice Poppa leaving the workroom.

She ignored the tinkling of the bell on the front door as customers came and went. But when the telephone rang, she heard a voice that wasn't Poppa's say, "Hello. Frank's Flowers." It was Yvonne!

Melody set down her shears and peeked into the shop.

Poppa was talking to a customer in front of the huge cooler full of dozens of different types of flowers and greenery. Yvonne was standing behind the counter near the cash register. She was wearing her best pleated skirt and stockings, and her straightened hair was held back by a headband.

"What are you doing here?" Melody asked after Yvonne hung up the phone.

Yvonne didn't look happy. "I'm taking a break from my summer job hunt."

"Why?"

"I applied for a job at the bank. The newspaper said

they were hiring students for the summer, but the manager didn't even look at my application."

"Maybe the jobs are all full, and they don't need anybody else," Melody suggested.

"That's what the manager told me, but it wasn't true. A white girl about my age went into his office after me, and I heard him say they still had several positions open."

"Is that the same bank where Mommy took me to open my savings account?" Melody asked.

Yvonne flushed angrily in answer. She looked as if she might cry.

Melody was outraged. "If they won't give my sister a job because she's black, then I'm going to take my money to a different bank."

Yvonne tried to smile. "Thanks, Dee-Dee."

"I'm serious," Melody said. The hurt on her sister's face made Melody think about something from a long time ago.

Once when Melody was only four and everyone else was already going to school, her grandparents had taken her south to see their cousins. It was very hot, and the lemonade in Big Momma's thermos was gone. Melody was still thirsty, so when Poppa stopped at a gas station in Alabama, Melody begged for a drink. There was a Coca-Cola machine, red and white and shiny. Poppa had given her a nickel so that she could buy a bottle of ice-cold soda pop. But when Melody started walking toward the vending machine, Big Momma had said, "Stop, baby."

"I want a drink!" Little Melody had said.

"I know," Big Momma had answered, "but we can't today. The machine is broken. Put your money in your pocket now."

Big Momma had taken Melody's hand to guide her away, and as Melody cried and followed, a little blonde girl about her size went to the machine. She stood on tiptoe and dropped a coin in. Then she reached in and pulled a frosty bottle out of the machine.

"It's not broken!" Melody had shouted. "It's not! I want a soda pop, too!" she'd cried, pulling against Big Momma's arm. Melody remembered crying for a long time, and none of Big Momma's other treats could make her feel better.

It wasn't until she was older and she could read that she understood. A few years later they were again driving south and again stopped at a gas station, this time in Tennessee. Melody saw the same kind of soda machine. There was a sign above the machine that said "Whites Only." That was when Melody realized that the machine in Alabama must have had the same kind of sign.

Melody had asked Big Momma why she hadn't told her about the sign the first time, in Alabama.

"Because it hurt me too much," Big Momma said.

"I didn't want it to hurt you, too."

Melody's memory faded as the bell on the door of the flower shop tinkled. She was determined to get her money out of that bank.

Two teenage boys had wandered into the store, and the girls turned their attention to them.

"You sell corsages?" one of them asked sheepishly.

Melody smiled. She knew that a corsage was a tiny flower arrangement that girls wore to dances and proms.

Yvonne looked very businesslike. "Yes," she said. "Are you looking for a corsage to pin on a dress, or for the girl to wear on her wrist?"

"I dunno," the boy said.

"How much do they cost?" the other boy asked.

"How much do you have?" Yvonne asked.

"One dollar!" they both said at the same time.

Yvonne rolled her eyes, and Melody tried not to laugh. One dollar wasn't enough money to buy a very fancy corsage. But she could tell that Yvonne had a plan. Poppa, who had finished with his customer, was watching.

"Well," Yvonne said, "we can give you a special prom deal. Two single carnations with two ribbons for one dollar! We'll even match the color of the ribbons to the young lady's dress."

Melody saw Poppa's eyebrows rise.

"For real?" The first boy was shocked.

"Tell your friends," Yvonne said. "I know there are three dances at different high schools next week. This special runs only till Wednesday."

"Cool! We'll spread the word! Do we pay now?" the second boy asked.

"Yes." Yvonne picked up a receipt book from the counter. Melody went over to her grandfather.

"Poppa, I think you should give Yvonne a job."

"I'm thinking the same thing, Little One," he said.

🎵

"Mommy!" Melody yelled as soon as she and Yvonne got home. "Mommy!"

The radio was playing a Smokey Robinson song when Melody burst into the kitchen. Her mother was snapping her fingers to the beat while she danced in front of the refrigerator. A stack of her students' math papers was on the kitchen table, and a pot of spaghetti sauce was bubbling on the stove.

"What in the world is it?" Mommy asked, putting a lid on the pot. She stopped dancing and turned down the sound on the radio.

"Yvonne didn't get a job, so I have to go to the bank!" Melody plopped into a chair.

"Explain," Mommy said, glancing at Yvonne. Yvonne

only shrugged and tilted her head toward Melody.

"Yvonne tried to get a job at the bank, but they wouldn't hire her because she's black." Melody was angry again just thinking about the whole thing. "I want to protest by taking my money out. Will you take me to the bank tomorrow?"

"Yes," Mommy said, without asking any other questions.

♪

The very next day after school, Melody held her mother's hand as they walked through the lobby of Detroit Bank. Melody had worn her best school jumper, and she carried her bank-account book. Melody looked around the large room. She and her mother were the only black people in sight, and she was the only child.

Melody and her mother stood in a short line, and for a few seconds Melody felt uncomfortable. Was everyone looking at her? Her cheeks were suddenly very warm, and her fingers felt sweaty as she curled them around her bankbook. *Can I do this?* Melody wondered. She had asked her mother in the car what to say and how to say it, but now Melody was nervous. Then she saw a girl Yvonne's age working behind a desk. She was white. Did she get a job when Yvonne couldn't even apply? Melody took a deep breath and reminded herself that she was standing up for her sister—and for making things fair.

When it was her turn, Melody let go of Mommy's hand and stepped up to the counter, which came up to her shoulders. Melody made herself as tall as she could.

The bank teller was an older white woman with red hair. "I would like to withdraw my money," Melody told her.

"And how much would you like to withdraw?"

"All of it."

The teller raised her eyebrows. "Are you sure?" she asked kindly.

"Yes," Melody said firmly. "My sister is really good with money and numbers, but this bank wouldn't let her apply for a summer job because she's black. That's not fair."

The teller looked confused for a moment. "Do you understand, dear, that if you withdraw everything, you'll close your account?" She glanced over Melody's head in Mommy's direction.

Melody slid her bankbook across the counter. Her insides were quivering, but she looked straight at the teller. "Yes. I understand. This bank discriminates against black people. I don't want to keep my money here anymore."

It seemed like forever before the woman finally nodded and picked up Melody's bankbook. Melody watched the teller count out ten one-dollar bills and put them into a

small envelope. Melody noticed that the girl behind the desk was staring with her mouth open, as if she didn't believe a kid could do something this important. Melody turned away.

Her mother smiled and took her hand. "Good job," she said. "You know, your daddy says voting is a way to speak up for what we believe. Money has a voice, too. What we do with it says a lot about what we believe."

Melody blew out a breath of relief. "Thanks, Mommy."

"I'm proud of you, Melody," her mother said as they walked out of the bank side by side.

Mother's Day Surprises

♪ **CHAPTER 5** ♪

Melody woke up early on Mother's Day. She got up and nudged Lila, who was snoring softly in her bed. "Get up! We've got to make breakfast for Mommy before church," she said. Melody looked over at her other sister's bed, but it was empty. Yvonne was already up.

Melody ran into Yvonne in the hall. Yvonne was coming out of the bathroom, tying a scarf over her head.

"Don't you usually take that *off* in the morning?" Melody whispered. Yvonne often wore the scarf to keep her hair from getting too tangled up while she slept.

Yvonne only nodded. "Let's get the Mother's Day surprises started," she whispered, waving Melody down the stairs.

In the kitchen, Yvonne made coffee. A few minutes later, Lila came down, dragging Dwayne by the arm.

"So early," he said sleepily.

Melody went outside to the garden she had planted along the driveway. Only a few spring flowers had bloomed, but she picked what was most beautiful and took the bunch back inside. She arranged the bright daffodils in a teacup and set it on the tray.

"Okay, everything is ready," Dwayne said. He picked up the tray, carefully carrying it up the stairs with his sisters and Bo following behind. At their parents' door, Melody knocked.

"Who is it?" Daddy said in his joking voice.

"It's me—I mean, it's us," Melody answered. "We're here with Mother's Day breakfast for Mommy."

"Come on," Daddy said.

Melody opened the door and with her brother and sisters sang *"Happy Mother's Da-a-ay . . ."* Bo jumped on the bed and started barking.

"That is wonderful!" Their mother clapped as Dwayne put the tray across her knees. "Thank you all."

While their mother ate, Melody, Dwayne, and Lila crowded onto the foot of the bed. "This certainly is an improvement over last year's Mother's Day breakfast," Daddy said, sneaking a bite of scrambled egg. "You delivered burnt pancakes."

Lila giggled. "That was Dwayne's fault."

"Oh, no it was *not*," Dwayne said. "That was Yvonne."

"Where *is* Yvonne?" Mommy asked.

Before anyone could answer, they heard water running in the bathroom. Melody looked at the clock on her parents' bedside table. "Lila! We have to get ready for church, too," she said, jumping off the bed.

An hour later, Melody and Lila were waiting in the living room. Both of them had on the white blouses and navy blue skirts that the girls in the children's choir wore whenever they performed. Dwayne came down wearing his dark suit and tie. Daddy called up the stairs. "Yvonne, this is not a beauty contest. This is church. We must go, or your sisters are going to be late."

"I'm coming!" Yvonne's voice floated downstairs.

Then came the biggest Mother's Day surprise. Yvonne walked slowly down the stairs. She wore an orange dress and carried a matching jacket. But as her entire body came into view, she was also wearing an Afro hairstyle. Her chin-length hair, which she usually straightened, was now a curly, crinkly globe standing out a few inches around her face.

Mommy gasped.

Dwayne chuckled.

"What did you do to your head?" Daddy asked in disbelief.

No one they knew had ever worn an Afro. Melody and Lila and all their friends

usually wore pigtails or braids so that their hair stayed neat, even when they ran around and played. Grown ladies like Mommy—and the Motown girl groups Melody admired— wore straightened hairstyles that were smooth and glossy and tidy. On special occasions, Melody got to wear her hair straightened, too.

"I'm going natural," Yvonne announced, putting her jacket on. "I'm honoring my African heritage. Happy Mother's Day, Mom. Do you like it?"

Mommy stared at Yvonne for a minute. "I . . . I don't really know how I feel yet," she said.

Melody reached up to touch her sister's hair. It was tightly curled, soft, and springy. "It's nice," Melody said. "It's like a crown."

When they all got into the station wagon, Dwayne complained that Yvonne's hair took up too much room. Daddy made him sit in the fold-down seat at the back.

As the Ellisons filed out of the car in front of the church, Melody heard whispers from the prim and proper ladies with straightened hair and fancy hats. "What sort of a hairdo is that?" one of them whispered to the others, not at all quietly. Melody knew that Yvonne heard them, too, but she just smiled. *She stands up for what she believes in,* Melody thought. *I'm so proud she's my sister.*

♪

At the end of the service, the children's choir sang for all the mothers. As the music started, Melody looked out and saw her mother in her usual seat right next to Big Momma. Both of their hats were nodding in time to the music. As Diane sang her solo, Melody kept her eyes on her mother and grandmother. When it was time for her to join in, she sang with love in every single note.

When the song ended, the congregation clapped and cheered. Pastor Daniels gave a single rose to each of the mothers. Melody and Yvonne had tied ribbons to each flower at Poppa's shop yesterday.

As the last roses were handed out, Melody noticed three people coming into the church. *Who would show up now?* Melody wondered. Then her eyes grew wide. It was Charles and Tish and Val! Val was wearing a frilly pink dress and pink socks with ruffles at the edges, and her hair was in a poufy ponytail tied up in a bow. There was Cousin Charles, tall and skinny, with a mustache and a beard like Poppa, and Cousin Tish, as tall as Charles. She wore a hat with a feather that made her seem even taller.

Melody sped down the side aisle and zigzagged around chatting grown-ups to get to the back.

"Val!" Melody squealed, crushing Val's Sunday dress as she gave her an enormous hug.

"Dee-Dee!" Val knocked Melody off balance as she hugged back.

"You said you were coming when school was out," Melody said.

"I thought we were. But Mama and Daddy decided to start packing right after I wrote to tell you we were moving," Val explained. "We left yesterday. Daddy drove all night so that we could get here in time for church." Then she laughed. "I guess we didn't quite make it."

"What a great surprise," Melody said, giving Val's hand a squeeze. "I'm so glad you're here!"

A Family Reunion

Melody didn't want Val out of her sight for even a moment, so after church, the girls rode together in the back of Big Momma and Poppa's car.

When Poppa pulled up to his house, Daddy, Dwayne, and Cousin Charles were already leaning against Charles's Ford Fairlane, talking and laughing. The mothers were walking slowly up the driveway, talking and laughing. Melody knew that the day was going to be full of talking and laughing.

"Look at you, man!" Charles thumped Dwayne on the back. "You got taller! Are you still singing?"

Melody saw Dwayne duck his head, but he answered, "Yeah, yeah I am."

"He's just playing with that music business in his spare time," Daddy said. "He's going to college in September."

Val pulled Melody up the walk. Big Momma and Cousin Tish were standing on either side of Yvonne on the porch steps, studying her Afro while Mommy looked on.

"Now, how did you get it to stand up?" Big Momma was asking.

"I have a special comb," Yvonne said.

"Some people don't like natural hair because it looks so different from what we're used to," Tish said. She had owned a hair salon in Birmingham, and she was looking at Yvonne thoughtfully. "I think that style suits your face," Tish said. "I'm going to open a salon here. I wonder if my future Detroit clients would like a style like that?"

"I'm not sure how many young women are as radical as our Yvonne," Mommy said, opening the front door.

"What does 'radical' mean?" Melody asked.

"It means somebody who's willing to raise her voice," Yvonne said.

"Willing to raise her hair, too!" Mommy said as she went inside.

Melody and Val followed, but they all bumped into a traffic jam. Everyone was looking up at the arch where Poppa had quickly hung Melody's colorful construction-paper banner all the way across, saying "Welcome Charles, Tish, and Val." Underneath, on a small round table, was the Mother's Day flower arrangement Melody had made at Poppa's shop.

"Oh!" Tish clapped. "Who made all this loveliness?"

"Melody did," Lila said as Melody made her way to the dining room with Val right behind.

"Thank you, honey!" Tish gave her a hug. "There's

nothing like being around family."

"Come on, everyone," Big Momma called. "Let's eat."

There was so much talking and laughing that dinner went on and on. Everyone was so busy catching up on cousins and old friends that Big Momma served a second round of cake and ice cream.

"Say, Frances!" Charles said, scraping the last of the crumbs off his plate. "This reminds me of the first time you made a triple-chocolate cake. It was kind of lopsided, remember?"

Mommy said. "Yes, I remember. I was a new wife, and I didn't bake very well."

"What your mother did was nothing to laugh at," Daddy said. "I had dreamed about chocolate cake when I was overseas during the war. Your mother and I saw one in the window of a bakery in Birmingham the day I got back."

"Did you buy it?" Melody asked.

Mommy poured more coffee for the grown-ups. "We tried," she said. "That bakery refused to serve Negroes. I was so angry that I decided to try to make the cake myself."

Daddy said, "There we were,

fighting for freedom for the world, and we didn't have it when we got back home."

"But you two were Tuskegee Airmen!" Dwayne said. "I mean, you got a medal, Dad!"

"Yes. I was the most highly trained mechanic in my unit. I kept those planes in top flying condition. But when I left the service, I couldn't get a job in my hometown. I had to move to Detroit and start at the bottom doing the most backbreaking jobs at the auto factory."

Charles sighed. "Things sure haven't changed much. Here I am, moving to Detroit for the same reason."

"What do you mean?" Melody asked.

"The black hospital where I worked closed down," Charles explained. "I tried to get a job at one of the white hospitals, but no one would hire me. I'm a licensed pharmacist, but it seemed as if people only saw me as a black man they couldn't be bothered with."

Melody thought about what had happened to Yvonne at the bank. "That's wrong," she whispered to her sister. Yvonne looked at Melody and nodded. So did Mommy.

Charles's face was serious. "I got stopped by a cop when I was on my way to a job interview. I was wearing a suit and tie, not doing anything wrong, but the police still treated me like a criminal. When the hospital closed, I just felt it was time for us to get out of Birmingham."

"But if everybody like you and Tish leaves, who's going to stay and fight?" Yvonne asked.

"Girl, if you miss a day of work to participate in a march or a protest, you can lose your job," Charles said. "I have a family to support. I couldn't risk it."

"But things are changing," Yvonne insisted.

"Yes, but things are also getting tense," Charles said. He put his coffee cup down. "It was bad enough when white people threw food at peaceful protesters or pulled them off their seats at a lunch counter. But now the police are setting dogs and fire hoses on people!"

Tish tapped her bright red fingernails on the table. "Charles and I have been talking about this for months. There's a lot of good happening in the South, but some of it is getting dangerous. The police turned those hoses on children. *Children!*"

Melody knew what Tish was talking about. Everyone did. It had happened last week, and news of it was still on the TV every night. Melody had seen black schoolkids in Birmingham, singing and marching peacefully. Then policemen chased them and turned giant hoses on them. The blasts of water were so strong that they knocked the children to the ground.

Melody glanced at Val, who was looking down at her dish of ice cream.

"Those police in Birmingham were wrong," Big Momma said. She reached over and gently raised Val's chin with her hand. "And those children were very brave."

"I don't see why we have to fight fire with fire, as the old saying goes," Mommy said. "Dr. King speaks against hatred and fear. He believes we can change hearts and laws without violence."

"He's coming to Detroit next month," Poppa said, "making a speech down at Cobo Hall."

Melody felt as if something big was happening right here at her grandparents' table. She wasn't quite sure what it was, but she had a feeling that some kind of change was in the air.

"I heard people at the flower shop talking about it," Yvonne said. "There's going to be a march. It's called the Walk to Freedom!"

"Yes, our union is marching," Daddy said. "We don't have the same sort of segregation as in the South," Daddy continued, "but we need more good jobs for black people here in Detroit."

"And better, less crowded schools for black children," Mommy added. "And fair housing laws."

"You make it sound like Detroit is a mess," Dwayne piped up. "Black people like Poppa have businesses—and Tish, you want to open a business, right? Well, you can!

And don't forget that this is where the music starts. Hitsville, U.S.A. Motown." Dwayne started snapping his fingers and humming a tune. Everyone around the table started laughing.

Daddy rolled his eyes at Dwayne, but he was smiling when he said, "I think we should all take part in the march as a family."

"Go, Daddy!" Yvonne clapped her hands.

"I don't know, Cousin," Charles said. "We're staying out of this marching business. I just want to get my family settled in. We're looking to get a fresh start here in Detroit."

There was silence for a moment. "I understand how you must feel," Mommy said gently, looking at Charles. Then she turned to Daddy. "I would like to hear what Dr. King has to say in person."

"That young man is a powerful preacher," Poppa said. "I'd like to hear him, too."

Big Momma motioned to Lila. "Put the date on my kitchen calendar, Lila. When is it, Will?"

"June twenty-third," Daddy said. "Whoever's going will meet right here, so we can walk to freedom together."

♪

After dinner, Melody and Val went out on the front porch. Melody sat down on the top step. Val hesitated a moment and then smoothed the skirt of her dress and sat down too. "Are you tired after the long car ride from Birmingham?" Melody asked.

Val shrugged. "Kind of," she said quietly. "Everything happened so fast with our move. I couldn't really say good-bye to my friends the way I wanted to." She sighed. "I just feel like I don't have a real home anymore. You wouldn't understand."

"Tell me what you mean," Melody said. She *wanted* to understand.

"Detroit isn't home," Val said. "Home's not home anymore either. I used to feel safe in Birmingham. Now there's always police, and people in the streets getting arrested. I knew one of those kids who got knocked down by the water hose. She said it was really scary."

"Wow," Melody said. She told Val what Pastor Daniels had said that morning about everybody deserving justice. "Those kids stood up for themselves. That's really brave."

"I know," Val said, looking at their reflections in the toes of her patent leather shoes. "But we're just kids."

"But we still count," Melody said. "This is our world,

too!" She told Val what she'd done at the bank when her sister couldn't get a job there.

"You were really brave," Val said.

Melody took her cousin's hand. "I promise to help you feel at home here," Melody said. Then she had an idea. "I'll take you to the library tomorrow, as soon as I'm done with school."

Val brightened a bit. "That sounds like fun," she said. "Where is the library?"

"Not far," Melody told her. "Only nine blocks."

Val looked shocked. "My mama and daddy didn't let me walk that far by myself in Birmingham. Not with everything that was going on."

Melody smiled. "Well, you're in Detroit now. And remember when Dwayne mentioned Motown? The studio is close to the library. We'll walk right by it. Maybe we'll even see somebody famous!"

Val slowly smiled back. "I think living in Detroit is going to be *real* interesting."

Signs and Songs

♫ CHAPTER 7 ♫

I t was finally June, and school was finally over. Melody burst through the front door of her house on the last day and tossed her book bag into a corner.

"I'm done, I'm done!" She did a little dance right on the living room rug while Lila came in behind her.

"Don't forget to pick that up," Lila told her before tromping up the stairs with her book bag thumping.

"I guess you're glad school is out," Yvonne said from the dining room.

Melody nodded. "Yes, but Sharon's going to New Orleans tomorrow for the whole summer, so I'm going to miss her." Melody stopped dancing. "I'm glad Val's here already. I can't wait to call her!"

"You don't have to wait," Val said as she appeared from the kitchen.

"You're here!" Melody laughed, rushing over to give her cousin a hug. "It has been so hard to sit in school knowing that you're done already."

"It's been just as hard waiting for y'all to finish!" Val said, sitting down at the dining room table. "Daddy's started his new job, and Mama's looking for a place for her salon, so I could use some company."

"Yvonne, how come you're not at the flower shop?" Melody asked.

"Poppa gave me the afternoon off to work on a special project," Yvonne said.

Melody noticed that the table was covered with poster boards, paints, crayons, and glue. "What are you making?"

"Signs for the Walk to Freedom," Val said proudly. "Look at the one I just painted."

Melody read the big blue words out loud. *"Freedom Forever."* There were other slogans, too. *Justice for All! Fair Housing Now! Separate Is Not Equal!* "Wow. This is really cool," Melody said.

Yvonne nodded. "We're making as many as we can. I'll take them to the church. Someone there will pass them out on the Sunday of the march."

Lila came back downstairs. She had changed out of her school clothes. "Oh, can I help?" she asked.

"Me, too?" Melody asked.

"Sure," Yvonne nodded. "But Melody, you'd better change out of your school clothes."

Melody hurried upstairs to put on a shirt and a pair of shorts. When she came back, Dwayne was stomping through the back door, singing "Summertime." He stuck his head into the dining room.

Melody was surprised to see him. He was usually still at the factory at this time of day. She looked at the clock and then at Dwayne. When she opened her mouth to say something, Dwayne pulled his finger and thumb across his lips. *This has something to do with his secret,* Melody thought. She didn't say a word.

"What's up with all this?" Dwayne asked.

"They're for the freedom walk," Melody told him.

"I am not going on any freedom walk," he said. "I've got better things to do."

"What could be more important than freedom?" Yvonne asked.

"Being lead singer of Dwayne and The Detroiters," he said.

Lila said, "You'd better be thinking about college, too. You know what Daddy says."

"Plenty of people do just fine without a college degree!" he said. "Look at Tish!" He went into the kitchen.

Val stopped tracing the word "Justice" and pointed her pencil at Lila. "My mama says it's just as important for a colored person to run a business as it is to go to college."

Yvonne smiled. "That's because Tish is a successful business owner."

"Like Poppa," Melody added.

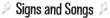

"And Berry Gordy at Motown. He's running a successful music business!" Dwayne called from the kitchen. A few minutes later, he came back into the dining room holding a saucer stacked with two peanut butter and jelly sandwiches. "Music is a *business*!"

"Bet you won't tell Daddy that," Lila said.

Dwayne rolled his eyes in her direction, and then nodded at Melody. "So how's *your* music coming?" he asked.

"My song?" Melody thought about her Youth Day solo all the time, but she still didn't know what she was going to sing. "I haven't picked one yet," she confessed.

Dwayne shoved the last corner of one of the sandwiches into his mouth and pulled Melody into the living room. As they sat down on the sofa, Dwayne asked, "You love singing, don't you?"

"Yes," she said.

"And you want to do this solo, don't you?"

"Yes!" Melody answered right away.

"The songs you sing don't just have to be right for your voice, okay? Your song has to *feel* right. The words have to mean something special to you. When they do, amazing things happen."

"Is that why all your songs are so good?" Melody asked.

Dwayne nodded. "I kind of think so."

Melody thought about that and said. "But how will I know which one song is right for me?"

"You'll know." Dwayne patted her shoulder. "You'll know when—"

Dwayne stopped talking when he heard their mother's key turn in the front door.

"Dwayne! Get off the sofa!" Melody whispered. "You're still in your work clothes."

He jumped up and quickly disappeared.

"I'm home!" Mommy called out the way she always did when she came in. "And I've brought company!"

Melody looked curiously at the older woman who followed Mommy in. Her hair was snow white and she walked with a wooden cane, but her dark face had no wrinkles at all. The woman's sharp dark eyes twinkled as she looked back at Melody.

"This is Miss Esther Collins. She's just joined our church, and she's helping me on the finance committee. Miss Esther, this is my youngest, Melody. And those are my other two daughters, Yvonne and Lila, and Cousin Valerie."

"Hello, Miss Esther!" the girls said.

"Please sit down while I get those phone numbers for you," Mommy said, going upstairs.

Instead of sitting, Miss Esther headed to the dining

room, clicking her cane across the floor. "You young people are always busy," she said. "What's this you're doing?"

"We're making posters for the Walk to Freedom," Melody told her.

"Oh, yes." Miss Esther nodded. "It's going to be quite an event. That young Dr. King is speaking."

Yvonne looked up, impressed. "You know about it?"

Miss Esther nodded. "We've been fighting this fight for a long time, child. You're never too old or too young to stand up for justice."

Melody smiled. Miss Esther had given her a great idea for the sign she would make for the march.

♫

A week later, Melody and Lila were in the kitchen eating bologna and cheese sandwiches and drinking ginger ale when they heard someone at the front door.

Lila stopped chewing. "Who in the world is that in the middle of the day?"

"Maybe Yvonne came home early," Melody said.

Before Lila could call out, the first notes of one of Dwayne's tunes came from their living room. Three male voices harmonized to the music.

"It's Dwayne and his group!" Lila whispered.

"Where's the music coming from? We don't have a piano," Melody whispered back.

Lila rolled her eyes. "Obviously they got a tape recorder from somewhere!" She got up and motioned for Melody to follow. The sisters stood at the kitchen door, listening.

The song was so lively that Melody started dancing to the beat. Then she bumped the butter knife that Lila had left on the counter, and it clattered to the floor. The music stopped.

In a second, Dwayne swung the kitchen door open. "Are you two snooping?"

"Sort of," Melody said.

Instead of getting upset, Dwayne shrugged. "So why don't you come on in? Be our audience."

Lila headed for the living room, but Melody held back and grabbed her brother's arm. "Shouldn't you be at work?" she asked. Melody was still keeping Dwayne's secret about the Motown audition. Now it seemed as if Dwayne was keeping a secret from her.

"I'll tell you later," he whispered. "I promise."

Melody followed him to the living room and plopped onto the couch beside Lila, who was talking to Artie and Phil. Dwayne, Artie, and Phil had been friends forever. For the last year, they'd been singing all over the city.

Dwayne seemed nervous as he said, "Okay. This is a song I wrote for us. Check out our sound."

Artie, Phil, and Dwayne lined up with their backs to

the sofa. Dwayne started the tape recorder. They all spun around. *"Never thought I'd see the day that you made me feel this way,"* they sang together. *"Everything was sun, now everything is rain."*

Dwayne stepped forward. *"Never, ever dreamed you'd cause me this much pain."*

At the last words, they all turned their backs to Melody and Lila again. The girls clapped and hooted and stomped their feet.

"Aw, come on!" Dwayne said happily, looking over his shoulder.

"Are you still going by the name of 'Dwayne and The Detroiters,'?" Lila asked. "You need something catchier."

Melody thought for a moment. "How about The Three Ravens? You could wear the same outfits, like The Temptations! Maybe black suits with matching purple shirts and ties." Melody hopped up from her seat. "And those moves aren't cool enough. What if you spin one at a time—kind of bend and swirl around, like this?" Melody demonstrated. "When Dwayne is singing, you guys can't stand still," she said. "The Motown guys really dance."

Phil and Artie were already nodding, trying some different steps.

"Yeah! Yeah!" Melody nodded. "What do you think, Dwayne?"

"I'm thinking I can't believe how good you are at this, Dee-Dee," Dwayne said. "I'm going to get us some Kool-Aid," he said to the other two Ravens. Then he motioned for Melody to follow him to the kitchen.

Dwayne took down the pitcher, and Melody got out two packets of the strawberry powder and a wooden spoon.

"Here's the thing," Dwayne said. "Dad thinks I'm still working day shifts, but I quit my job at the factory."

"So that's why you're always coming and going!"

Dwayne nodded. "I got a part-time gig as a janitor down at Cobo Hall," he said. "Now I have more time to write music and rehearse with the guys."

Melody frowned. "Daddy's going to be really mad! You promised him you'd work at that factory until college started."

Dwayne shook his head. "I'm not cut out for factory work, Dee-Dee. Phil and Artie and I have a chance to make it big." He turned on the water to fill the pitcher.

Melody looked down at the swirling red liquid. Dwayne seemed so sure that he was right! Just like Yvonne always did. Melody wished she had their kind of courage.

"Listen," he said, turning back to her. "It's not gonna be easy—I'm not fooling myself. But we can sell records, lots of them. And I believe that when people hear our sound, they won't care what color our skin is."

Melody hadn't known that was how Dwayne felt. "Maybe if you explain that to Daddy, he'll understand. I could tell him—"

"No!" Dwayne said quickly. "Promise you won't say anything to Dad. We're gonna knock 'em out at our audition. I just know it. Then I'll tell Mom and Dad."

Melody stirred the Kool-Aid slowly. "I'm not going to tell a lie, you know."

"I know," Dwayne said, putting a hand on her shoulder. "And I would never ask you to do that. Just don't volunteer any information, okay?"

"I guess."

"There's one more thing," he said. "I need a new suit for the audition. Would you go shopping with me, since you seem to know just what I should be wearing?"

Melody couldn't help but smile. "All right to everything," she said. "Especially you telling Daddy soon. But . . ."

"But what?"

"Once I pick a song for Youth Day, you help me, too."

"You got it! Whatever you need." Dwayne picked up the spoon to continue stirring.

The Power Inside

On Saturday morning, Dwayne and Melody ate Cheerios together and then got ready to go shopping. Big Momma always said, "Look like you have money in your pocket when you go into a store," so Dwayne brushed his hair and put on a shirt with a collar. Melody wore a school skirt and borrowed Lila's shoulder purse. She took two of the one-dollar bills that she had gotten when she closed her account at the bank and tucked them into the purse. Melody told Dwayne she had decided to buy herself something special to wear for her Youth Day solo. She was excited that they both had something to shop for.

Dwayne whistled a tune but didn't say much as they walked. A few blocks from home, they turned onto 12th Street, which was lined with shoe shops, dress stores, and other businesses.

Fieldston's Clothing was one of the older stores on the street. Poppa had often told them how he had bought his first city suit there when he moved to Michigan from Alabama. When he opened his flower shop several years later, there were only a few businesses owned by black people in the neighborhood. Even though Mr. Fieldston was white, he'd given Poppa lots of good advice. Now Mr. Fieldston was long gone, and someone else ran the store.

A bell chimed as Dwayne held the door open for Melody. There were three clerks chatting at the front counter, but none of them said, "May I help you?" or even "Hello." All the clerks were white, and they were all wearing blue jackets. As she and Dwayne began to look around, Melody noticed several other shoppers, but she and her brother were the only black customers.

"The men's suits are over here," Dwayne said, nodding to the left. "But you'll want to see what's over there," he said, motioning to the right.

Melody saw a display of women's jewelry, and she smiled. "I'll just look for a few minutes," she told Dwayne. "Then I'll come and help you."

Melody wandered through the aisles of clothing racks and display cases, her shoulder purse swinging. She stopped to admire some silky scarves. Melody wrapped one around her neck, turning to find a mirror so that she could see how she looked. She almost bumped into one of the store clerks. "Excuse me," Melody said to the woman politely. The woman didn't say anything, but she watched as Melody took the scarf off and put it neatly back where she'd found it.

Melody walked over to a glass case filled with neck-laces. As she leaned closer, she saw the reflection of a man standing behind her. Thinking that he was looking too, she moved out of his way and on to a rack of barrettes. *Maybe I should get these instead of a headband,* she thought. She was about to take a pair from the rack when she changed her mind. She turned and saw the same man from the jewelry display. He looked at her suspiciously. Suddenly, Melody felt uncomfortable. She hurried over to Dwayne, no longer excited about shopping for herself.

Dwayne was holding up two black jackets. "How about one of these?" he asked.

"Oh! That's the one you need," Melody said, pointing to the one with shiny gold buttons.

A young man came toward them carrying an armful of boxes. Dwayne held up the jacket with the shiny buttons. "Excuse me, what's the price on this?"

The man with the boxes gave Dwayne an annoyed look and brushed roughly past without answering. Dwayne shrugged and slipped the jacket on. Melody nodded her approval. It seemed to fit perfectly. Dwayne looked at the edge of the sleeve for a price tag, and then held his arm up high. "Can I get a price on this, please?"

"You can't afford it," a man said.

Melody turned to see the same man who'd stood

behind her at the necklaces and the barrettes. Had he followed her?

"Take it off," the man said coldly.

"I have money," Dwayne said, frowning.

Melody looked toward the front counter. Mommy always said to ask nicely for a manager if you had trouble in a store.

The man shook his head, and Melody noticed that he was wearing the same blue jacket as all the other clerks.

She suddenly suspected that he hadn't been standing behind her by mistake.

"I can guess what your kind really came in here for," he hissed.

"What do you mean?" Melody asked. "What's he talk-ing about?" she whispered to Dwayne. Then she saw a look cross Dwayne's face—a look she'd never seen before. It was like anger and fear and something else all mixed together. Dwayne slowly took off the jacket and carefully hung it back on the rack, shaking his head.

"Wait," Melody said, tugging at her brother's arm. "You need a suit."

"Not at this price," Dwayne said quietly.

"I've had enough of your type," the clerk said. "Get out. And take your little shoplifting companion with you." His eyes flashed right at Melody.

"Shoplifting?" Melody's mouth dropped open. "That's not true," she protested. "We didn't steal anything," she said louder, her heart pounding. "We're just shopping like everybody else!"

"Dee-Dee," Dwayne didn't raise his voice. "Let's go."

"You'd *better* go. Get out, before I call the cops!" the man shouted.

Melody realized with a sinking feeling that the man who was shouting was the manager. Dwayne was pulling her toward the door. She didn't want to stay, but she couldn't move. How could that man have accused her of doing something so horrible? As they left the store, Melody knew that Mommy had been wrong. That manager would never have helped them. He was the trouble.

Outside, Dwayne wouldn't look at Melody. He started walking so quickly that Melody had to run to keep up with him. She brushed away tears. Her insides were shaky, as if she'd just escaped something dangerous. Melody wanted to ask her brother if he was as upset as she was, and what he would do about his audition suit. "Dwayne?"

He spun around so quickly that she had to step back.

His face was like a mask, as if he didn't feel anything at all.

"Should we go tell Poppa?" Melody asked.

Dwayne shook his head. "That won't help. Besides, this isn't the first time something like this has happened to me, and it won't be the last time."

Melody stood very still. Would that happen to her again? Would she be accused of shoplifting when she was just shopping? Then Melody felt a prickle of fear for her brother. What if the store clerk had called the police? Who would the police have believed, Dwayne or the clerk?

Melody took a deep breath. "Yvonne says we have to change things. That's why we have to march! That's why we're walking with Dr. King next Sunday."

Dwayne put his hand on Melody's shoulder. "I don't think a march is going to change things for me. Don't you see now? I have to use my talent to become a famous singer if I want things to be different."

Would people really treat Dwayne fairly if he was famous? Melody wondered. "I understand that you want to be famous," she said. "And I believe in you, Dwayne . . ."

"But?"

"But what about everyone else? Shouldn't we try to change things for people who aren't ever going to be famous? People who are just ordinary, like me?"

Dwayne cracked a half smile. "Now you sound like

Yvonne. The answer is yeah, everybody has to work to make things different. But we don't have to do it the same way. Everybody's got the power for change inside themselves. Music is mine."

Melody was shaken by what had happened in the store. But the idea that everybody had some great power inside made her feel more hopeful than she had felt just a few minutes ago.

"By the way, Dee-Dee," Dwayne said quietly, "you are not ordinary."

"I'm not?"

"Nothing close. I can't wait to see how you're gonna change the world, girl."

♪

Melody wanted to go to Big Momma's house, so Dwayne walked her there. He didn't talk much, and he left right away to meet his friend Artie.

Big Momma was finishing a lesson in the living room, so Melody went into the kitchen and closed the door. She couldn't get the shouting store manager out of her head, so she turned the radio on softly, hoping that the music would take her mind off what had just happened.

Melody sat down at the kitchen table as a Smokey Robinson song ended. The DJ on the local station started reporting details about the upcoming freedom walk.

"Here's a song you're likely to hear during the walk," the announcer said. "'Lift Every Voice and Sing.' Often called the Negro national anthem, a colored man, James Weldon Johnson, wrote the lyrics as a poem, and his brother wrote the music."

Melody had always liked the title, and now, as the song began to play, she realized that it said what she was feeling inside. At that moment, Melody knew it was exactly what she wanted to sing for Youth Day.

When Big Momma was finished with her lesson, Melody went out to the living room. "Big Momma, could you play 'Lift Every Voice and Sing'?" Melody asked. She wasn't surprised when her grandmother went to the piano and started to play without any sheet music.

"What are the lyrics?" Melody asked. She had heard the song many times, but now she wanted to hear all the words.

Big Momma stopped playing. "I have the music right here," she said. She stood and opened her piano bench and looked through several sheets of music. Then she handed Melody an old songbook.

"Lift every voice and sing, till earth and heaven ring." Melody read the first line and imagined being able to sing out, loud and strong, so the whole world could hear.

"Would you play it again, please?" Melody asked.

Big Momma sat down again. Melody propped the book

on the piano and then stood close to Big Momma, reading the words silently as she followed the music. When
the song ended, Melody felt the most wonderful feeling
stirring inside her.

"Just in case you want to know," Big Momma whispered, "no one has ever sung this at a Youth Day concert
before."

The Walk to Freedom

♪ CHAPTER 9 ♪

Melody couldn't get the tune of "Lift Every Voice and Sing" out of her mind. All week she'd carried around the songbook Big Momma had given her. She'd memorized all three verses, and on the afternoon of the freedom walk, she was thinking hard about the words.

"Vonnie," Melody asked, "what does it mean to *ring with the harmonies of liberty*?" She could see her sister's face in the mirror over the dresser. Yvonne finished smoothing Melody's hair before she answered.

"Harmony is everybody joining together."

"Is that playing nicely, like Mommy used to tell us?"

"Right. And liberty—"

"Means free. I know. Like the Pledge of Allegiance."

"That's a really important song you're learning, Dee-Dee," Yvonne told her, adjusting Melody's headband.

"Why?"

"Well . . ." Yvonne wrinkled her face in thought. "It's about the future, really. I mean, most black Americans are relatives of people who were brought to this country in chains. Slavery went on for two hundred and fifty years.

And even though last January was the one hundredth anniversary of the Emancipation Proclamation that outlawed slavery, black people today are still being oppressed."

Melody spun around in her chair. "Oppressed?"

"It means held back. You know, not allowed to shop where they want or get the jobs they want or live where they want. Not allowed to really be free."

Yvonne put Melody's brush down on the dresser and picked up the big fork-like comb that she used for her Afro. "So, see?" she continued. "This song encourages us to remember how strong we were in the past, but also pushes us to keep being strong now, to keep fighting every day until—"

"Until earth and heaven ring." Melody said. She was beginning to understand. "And that means never giving up until everything is fair, doesn't it?"

Yvonne patted Melody on her shoulders and said, "Liberty and justice is for all, little sis. That's why kids in the South march, that's why I help folks register to vote, and that's why we're walking in Detroit today."

Melody thought back to how the man at Fieldston's had treated her and Dwayne so unfairly. Melody wanted the Walk to Freedom to keep things like that from happening in the future.

"Melody," Daddy called up the stairs. "It's time to go."

"What about you?" Melody asked Yvonne.

"I'm riding with friends," Yvonne explained.

When Melody got downstairs, Poppa and Big Momma were in the living room. Everyone got into the station wagon. As Daddy drove along Woodward Avenue, Melody saw hundreds of people heading downtown on foot.

"This is like going to the Hudson's Thanksgiving Day parade," Lila said. "Look at the crowds!"

Melody perked up. She saw some people carrying flags and others waving signs that looked just like the ones she and Lila had helped make.

"This traffic is something awful," Poppa said. "Will, maybe we'd better park the car and start walking already." Daddy didn't argue. He pulled over at the next empty spot along the curb.

"I see a group from New Bethel Baptist Church," Mommy said. "Reverend C. L. Franklin is pastor there. He helped organize the walk and bring Dr. King to speak." She stopped to tie a scarf over her hair and put on sunglasses.

"I hear a band," Lila said.

Melody strained to hear, but the music was too far away for her to recognize the tune. She looked up at the clear blue sky and at the crowd gathering from all the side streets. This was different from a parade.

Daddy opened the back of the station wagon and pulled out two neatly lettered signs. One said "Down With Discrimination." The other read "Stand Up For Justice."

"That's the one I made," Melody said proudly.

"I believe there are thousands of folks out here," Mommy said as she took Melody's hand.

Poppa nodded. "More than they predicted on the radio."

Cobo Hall was the biggest auditorium in Detroit, built next to the Detroit River. People flowed slowly toward Cobo as if they had become a river, and the river sang.

Melody listened. She knew the song, and she opened her mouth to join in, just as Big Momma did, too. Together they sang

> *We shall not,*
> *We shall not be moved.*
> *We shall not,*
> *We shall not be moved.*
> *Just like a tree that's standing by the water,*
> *We shall not be moved.*

Big Momma took Melody's other hand. Walking there, between her mother and her grandmother, raising her girl voice with theirs, Melody felt strangely light, as if she could fly if they let go of her hands. And all the other voices surrounding them were like hearts beating together. *This is harmony,* Melody thought.

The sea of bodies slowed even more and then stopped. Melody couldn't see Cobo Hall. She knew they were still far away from the entrance.

"This is as close as we're going to get," Poppa said.

"At least we'll be able to hear the speeches," Daddy said. "They've got loudspeakers set up."

The speakers crackled, and the singing faded. A man began to speak. Melody's legs were tired, and she wondered when Dr. King would preach.

Then the roar of applause rose around them. Melody heard a different man's voice, a strong, clear, Southern voice. At last it was Dr. King! He talked about Abraham Lincoln and the Emancipation Proclamation that freed Negroes from slavery. He talked about Birmingham and how racial segregation was wrong.

Melody didn't understand everything Dr. King said, but she felt the excitement of the crowd around her as they shouted out "Yes!" at certain parts of his speech. The words took on a rhythm, and he was almost chanting.

"I have a dream," he said. "With this faith I will go out with you and transform dark yesterdays into bright tomorrows . . ." Melody's insides began to shiver as she thought of the words to "Lift Every Voice and Sing":

> *Sing a song, full of the faith*
> *that the dark past has taught us*
> *Sing a song full of the hope*
> *that the present has brought us*

All of her family's stories flashed through Melody's mind: Poppa leaving his farm, Mommy making the triple-chocolate cake because Daddy couldn't buy one, Yvonne being turned away at the bank, Dwayne being treated badly at Fieldston's.

Poppa had moved to Detroit and opened his flower shop—where Yvonne now had a summer job. Now Mommy made the best cake ever, and Dwayne was determined to succeed in a music career so that he would be treated fairly. None of them had ever given up hope. Melody felt inspired.

Dr. King was chanting, "Free at last! Free at last!" The applause was like thunder in the sunshine.

♪

On the walk back to the car, Melody made an announcement. "For Youth Day, I'm going to do 'Lift Every Voice and Sing.'"

"That's a big song for you, Little One!" Poppa said with a smile. She saw Mommy nodding her approval.

"Yes, it is," Melody said to him. "But when I hear it, I feel the way I did listening to Dr. King. That's how I want the audience to feel when I sing at Youth Day. Dwayne says when the words mean something special to a singer, amazing things happen."

Big Momma gave Melody's hand a squeeze. "Your brother is right. And I believe my chick can do anything she sets her mind to."

Fireworks

♪ CHAPTER 10 ♪

Melody was dreaming that she was on top of Cobo Hall singing "Lift Every Voice and Sing." But when she woke up, it wasn't singing she heard but the sound of her parents' voices. Melody sniffed the wisps of hickory smoke wafting through the open window. It was the Fourth of July. Daddy had the entire day off from work, and Melody knew he was up already, tending the barbecue.

Melody hopped out of bed and hurried to get dressed. Lila and Yvonne were both still asleep, but Melody was eager to get ready. She ran downstairs with Bo at her heels and swung around the post at the end of the banister. Melody stopped short when she saw her cousin Val sitting on the sofa. "You're here already!" Melody said happily.

"My daddy came over to help your daddy, and I came along," Val said. Bo rushed over to her, and Val scratched him behind the ear.

Melody grinned. "Well let's go see what the daddies are doing outside." She and Val sped through the dining room and burst into the kitchen. Mommy was wearing her red-white-and-blue-striped blouse and dancing to the radio.

"Happy Fourth of July, girls!" Mommy said. She was holding a bowl full of lemons that had been cut in half. "You're just in time to start the lemonade! Daddy put the big crock outside on the picnic table." She handed Val the bowl and Melody a juicer.

Melody crossed the cool linoleum of the kitchen and pushed the back door open. Daddy heard it creak and waved his tongs. Melody smiled. No matter how late her father worked on the day before the Fourth of July, he was always standing at his grill as soon as the sun came up.

Cousin Charles was busy setting up folding tables and chairs around the yard. He was wearing the baggiest shorts that Melody had ever seen. She held back a giggle.

"Aren't Daddy's shorts the ugliest?" Val whispered as she and Melody sat down at the picnic table.

"Yep," Melody laughed. The girls got to work, taking turns juicing the lemons.

Mommy came outside as the girls finished the lemonade and gave them ears of corn to shuck. Val picked up an ear, peeled the leaves off, and started singing into the corn as if it was a microphone.

Melody laughed, and then she had an idea. "Hey, let's put on a show today! You and Lila and I could pretend to be The Vandellas or The Marvelettes."

"That's a great idea!" Val said.

"I bet Yvonne would help us dress up," Melody added.

"Really?" Val said. "Let's go ask her!"

♪

Around two in the afternoon, when the Ellison's backyard was full of family and friends, Melody, Val, and Lila were upstairs. Yvonne was piling her bed with some dresses she'd outgrown.

Val sifted through the dresses on the bed. "I like this one!" she said, grabbing a blue dress. "And look at this, Dee-Dee! It's perfect for you!" Val held up a flowered dress with a bow at the waist.

Melody couldn't believe her eyes. "Can I really wear that one, Vonnie?" Yvonne hadn't worn the dress for years, but she hadn't ever let Lila or Melody wear it, either.

"For today," Yvonne answered. "Yes."

"Which Marvelettes song should we do?" Melody asked, holding the dress up in front of her. It was a little bit big, but they could pin it if they needed to.

"How about 'Please Mr. Postman'?" Yvonne suggested, sweeping Melody's hair up on top of her head. "You girls sing that all the time."

Val was tipping awkwardly in a pair of Yvonne's high heels. "*C'mon, deliver the letter, the sooner the better,*" she sang as Yvonne poked Melody's hair with bobby pins.

Once Yvonne finished pinning and piling hair and but-toning and zipping dresses, Melody, Val, and Lila twirled in front of the full-length mirror. Melody couldn't help grinning at what she saw. They weren't wearing matching dresses, but they still looked like Motown stars!

The girls hurried down to the kitchen, and Dwayne hushed the crowd in the backyard. "Ladies and gentlemen," he announced as the girls and their dresses floated onto the back stoop. "Introducing the Even More Marvelous Marvelettes!"

Melody giggled at the name Dwayne had invented. She fidgeted with the bow on her dress, but she wasn't one bit nervous. Already the music was inside her head, and her feet began to move.

"Music!" Lila ordered.

Dwayne and his band-mates started doo-wopping the song, and Melody, Val, and Lila began singing. Melody put her heart into having a good time. By the end of the song, she was dancing and waving her arms along with Val and

Lila. Other people were dancing, too, including her parents, Charles and Tish, and even Poppa and Big Momma.

"Encore!" Dwayne yelled when they finished. "That means one more time!" The girls sang the song again, and everyone in the backyard joined in.

Finally breathless, Melody and Val collapsed on the steps. Tish handed each of them a cold bottle of Vernor's ginger ale.

"That was so much fun," Val said.

Lila joined them. "I am starved!" she said, biting into a hot dog. "You'd better get one. Dad says he's running out of charcoal."

Val and Melody headed for the grill. Her father pressed a plump hot dog into a bun and handed it to Melody. "Nice job, daughter," he said, smiling. "I know you'll do the same on Youth Day."

"Thanks, Daddy."

Melody's father wiped sweat from his forehead and handed Charles his long grilling fork. "This crowd is still hungry. If you man the grill, I'll go for more charcoal."

"You got it," Charles agreed.

"I'm hot!" Val said when they finished their hot dogs. "Let's go out front and see if there's a cooler breeze."

The girls were on the front porch when Daddy returned. He got out of the car and slammed the door so hard that both girls jumped. "Is your brother still here?" he said in a low voice.

Melody nodded. "Yes, Daddy."

Her father didn't even get the charcoal out of the car. He stomped past them and into the backyard.

"What happened?" Val asked.

"I think something bad," Melody said, the fun of the day fading. She heard Daddy yelling for Dwayne. The back door opened and closed, and Melody heard Dwayne and her parents in the living room.

Melody told Val, "I'll be back," and went inside.

"I just ran into Joe Walker at the store," Daddy was saying. "He says you're a part-time janitor at Cobo Hall. He says you work a few hours in the afternoons. I want to know how you can be a day janitor at Cobo Hall when you're working a day shift at the factory."

Dwayne dropped his head. "I'm not working at the factory anymore, Dad."

"What?" Mommy said. She sounded shocked. Dwayne sighed. "I quit the factory a while ago. I needed more time for writing and rehearsing, and—"

"Rehearsing!" Daddy said angrily. "Boy, what is wrong with you? You know how hard it is for a Negro to get his foot in the door at that factory? You could have a steady job every summer when you're home from school!"

"Dad, I don't want my foot in that door." Dwayne wasn't shouting. He was calm. "I don't want to work at the factory. I don't want to go to college. I want a music career!"

"You promised us that you'd work at the factory and then go to college," Mommy said.

"I'm sorry, Mom. Dad. I can't keep that promise. I've got an audition at Motown next Thursday with my band. This is my chance. I have to try."

Daddy narrowed his eyes as he stood almost nose to nose with Dwayne. Melody held her breath.

"I'll pack my stuff," Dwayne said.

Melody exchanged a worried glance with her mother.

"I didn't ask—" Daddy began.

Dwayne put one hand on his father's shoulder and looked directly at him. "I know you didn't, Dad. But if Mr. Gordy likes us, he'll send us on the road right away to see how we perform for real audiences. I'll go stay at Phil's." He held out his other hand for a handshake.

Daddy looked down at Dwayne's hand and then back up at his face. In slow motion, he shook Dwayne's hand.

Dwayne looked at Mommy. "I can't be somebody I'm not," he said. "I'll make it work, Mom." Dwayne turned on his heel and bounded up the stairs.

Daddy shook his head. "If he thinks factory work is hard, wait until he learns what that music business is like.

I know some fellows who tried going down that road. It was too tough, and they couldn't make it."

Melody's parents went through the kitchen and out the back door, talking all the way outside. *Dwayne will make it work,* Melody told herself, trying not to cry. She sat on the bottom stair to make sure her brother didn't leave without saying good-bye. He didn't take long to come down.

"Melody, look. I didn't mean for things to happen like this."

Melody bit her lip. "Will you ever come home again?"

"If you're trying to tell me good-bye, forget it, sis," Dwayne said. "I'm gonna keep turning up, when you least expect me."

Melody looked down at her toes. "You won't be here to help me get ready for Youth Day."

"I'm sorry about that. You don't really need me, though. Big Momma has you covered. You listen to her. You'll be all right." He stood up. "I gotta go. Tell the sister-things I'll catch them later. And be good."

As soon as Dwayne had gone and closed the door behind him, the house felt different to Melody. Without Dwayne, her family was off-key.

Melody sat inside for a long time. When she finally went back outside, the sun had set and many people had left. Her grandparents were still there, sitting side by side under a tree in the deepening dusk.

Big Momma motioned for Melody to come over to them. "How are you feeling about your brother?" Big Momma asked.

"Kind of down," Melody said.

"Dwayne needs growing-into-a-man space," Poppa said. "He has to leave home to find it."

Big Momma said, "One day, you'll need growing-into-a-woman space, and you'll leave home, too. But for now, I say it's time for you to lift that beautiful instrument of yours. We'll start on Monday. Ten o'clock sharp."

Practice

♫ **CHAPTER 11** ♫

On the Monday after the Fourth of July, Melody was at her grandparents' house at exactly 9:59 a.m. Val was there to watch.

"Valerie," Big Momma said, "Melody needs to concentrate. Go on in the kitchen, darlin'."

Val gave Melody an encouraging smile and then pushed open the swinging door to the kitchen.

"Let's start at the beginning. Key?" Big Momma played a note, and Melody adjusted her voice by singing "Ahhh."

Melody had only sung a few words when they were interrupted by a furious knocking at the door. When Big Momma stopped playing and got up to answer it, Melody was surprised to see Diane Harris.

"Mrs. Porter! My mother got my lesson time mixed up, and—" Diane's frantic explanation squeaked to a halt when she noticed Melody. The girls just stared at each other.

"Mistakes happen, Diane," Big Momma said. "You'll have your lesson after Melody's. Come on in and pass right through to the kitchen. Melody's cousin Valerie is there, and you can sit with her."

Big Momma sat back down at the piano as if nothing had happened. Melody exhaled, trying to focus on the Walk to Freedom and how inspired she'd been after hearing Dr. King speak. She wanted people to feel the same way when they heard her sing this song.

She sang the entire first verse, but she didn't always hit the right notes. It was hard to keep up with the tempo because of the way the music swooped up and down, especially in the middle. Melody anxiously watched her grandmother's face for a sign of how she was doing.

Big Momma stopped playing. "Again," she said. "From the beginning."

For half an hour, Melody sang. Big Momma stopped frequently to give Melody direction. Melody had to sing one line over and over again. Finally, Big Momma closed her music book.

"Good," she said. "We have to work on tempo. Your lyrics aren't quite keeping pace with the music. And you have to make your voice sound bigger."

Melody nodded. "Lift it, you mean."

Big Momma handed Melody a cassette tape. "I made you this tape recording yesterday so you will have music to work with at home," Big Momma said. "You've given yourself a real challenge, but I know you'll conquer it. We'll practice again on Wednesday."

Melody twirled herself to the kitchen door, only remembering as she pushed it open that Diane was there.

"That was the Negro national anthem," Diane said. "Are you singing that for Youth Day?"

"Yes," Melody said, wondering what bossy Diane would say next.

"I never would have picked such an important song." Diane paused. "I would have picked something . . . safe."

Melody looked at Diane as if she was seeing her for the first time. "You're saying you would have been *scared* to try this song?"

Diane stood up from the table. "I only like to do what I'm good at. You're braver than I am."

"But you're always so confident," Melody said. "You're such a good singer! You're always singing solos at church."

"Miss Dorothy picked you to do the Youth Day solo," Diane said. "That's because *you're* such a good singer!"

Melody was speechless. *Did Diane Harris just compliment my voice?*

"Maybe it's possible that you're *both* good singers!" Val said. There was a pause, and then the girls burst out laughing.

Diane took a step toward the living room. "It's time for my lesson. I'll see you both next week?" she asked shyly.

"Yes!" Melody and Val answered together.

After Diane left, Melody looked at Val. "What did you say to her?"

Val laughed. "It wasn't anything I said. It was what you sang, Dee-Dee."

♪

On Thursday evening, Melody and her sisters were waiting anxiously to hear about Dwayne's audition. Mommy was still at a church meeting when the phone finally rang around nine o'clock. Yvonne answered it, and Dwayne asked to speak to their father. Daddy had worked a full day's shift and was asleep already, but Yvonne went to wake him up.

Melody and Lila hurried up the stairs after her and huddled outside their parents' bedroom with Yvonne so they could listen.

"Say what?" Daddy said, sounding sleepy. "What do they pay you for that? What? You would've done better on the assembly line. I'm going to sleep." There was a pause and then Daddy said, "You watch yourself out there." Daddy slammed the phone down. "All you sisters! Your brother is working for Motown. Good night!" In a few minutes, Daddy was snoring as loudly as the car engines he helped build at the Ford factory.

"Wow," Melody said. "Dwayne is making his dream come true."

Never Give Up

On a hot morning in August, Melody found Yvonne in the kitchen making sandwiches—lots of them. Everything was spread across the kitchen table.

"Who are all these sandwiches for?" Melody asked.

"They're for the group taking the bus trip down to D.C.," Yvonne said. "We're leaving tonight, and everybody's bringing food to share. Want to help wrap the sandwiches in wax paper?"

Melody nodded. "Are you excited about the march?" Yvonne was going to another freedom march, but this one was in Washington, D.C.

"Yes, I am!" Yvonne's earrings dangled as she nodded. "There will be thousands of people at the march, and a crowd that big will force government officials to listen to black people and change the laws all over the country."

"Will it be bigger than the freedom walk?"

Yvonne smiled. "Maybe. I bet all the TV news programs will cover it. Dr. King will be speaking, too."

Melody remembered how moved she'd been at the freedom walk and how Dr. King's speech had helped her begin to understand "Lift Every Voice and Sing."

Melody stacked a wax-paper-wrapped square on top of four others. "And then you're going back to school," she said.

"I'm sorry I won't be here for Youth Day," Yvonne replied. "I expect you to write and tell me everything, okay?"

"I will."

"And I will send you a postcard from D.C.," Yvonne said, setting the stacks of sandwiches in the refrigerator.

Melody sighed. "I can't believe the summer's almost over."

Yvonne put her arm around Melody's shoulders. "Time goes fast when you're doing important work."

♪

"Lila!" their mother called from the kitchen. "Have you got the television on?" Melody was already on the sofa with Val and her father. Daddy had stayed up after dinner on a work night especially to watch.

"Yes, Mom!" Lila was standing at the TV, turning channels.

"Stop there," Daddy said.

"Good evening," the announcer said. "Today, Wednesday, August 28, 1963, Washington, D.C., has seen what may be the largest gathering of peaceful civil rights marchers in the country's history."

Mommy squeezed in next to Melody, while Lila plopped down on the rug. Everyone stared intently at the television screen, which showed a big white building with a row of columns along its front.

"Hey, that's the Lincoln Memorial!" Lila said.

The image on the screen changed, and Melody gasped at the huge mass of people gathered in front of the building. It was the biggest crowd she'd ever seen. The TV camera was way up high—it must have been in an airplane—so the people looked like thousands of tiny moving shapes.

"Oh, let's look for Yvonne," Val said, bouncing on the sofa.

"No way will we see her in that crowd," Daddy said.

The TV screen switched to a close-up of the marchers. The people were black, white, Asian, and other races, too. They were young and old. Then the screen showed Dr. Martin Luther King Jr., who was at the top of some high steps in front of them all. "I have a dream!" he was saying.

Melody's mouth dropped open. "He said that at the freedom walk!"

"Shhh!" Her mother patted her knee.

Melody listened, feeling trembly and strange inside. It was just as Yvonne had said. There were so many people marching for fairness and justice that a TV camera in an airplane couldn't get a picture of all of them at once!

"Will you look at that," Daddy said, smiling. "All kinds of people coming out for justice! This—this is history, girls. Our history."

Melody thought, *Surely someone will hear their voices this time.*

One Sunday

♪ **CHAPTER 13** ♪

School began the first week of September, and everyone settled into a new routine. Dwayne was still traveling with The Three Ravens, and Yvonne wouldn't be home from Tuskegee until Thanksgiving. Val walked to school with Melody, Lila, and Sharon every day.

Melody was feeling more confident about her Youth Day performance. Choir practice had begun again, and Miss Dorothy kept saying how pleased she was that the choir was working together. Now that Melody had gotten to know Diane better, Diane was being a lot nicer—both at school and in the choir.

On the third Sunday of September, Melody, Lila, and Val sang together in the children's choir. Afterward, Poppa and Big Momma stayed at church for a meeting, but everyone else headed to their house for dinner. The men were outside looking at Charles's new car, and Mommy and Tish were talking in the kitchen. Lila was upstairs reading. Melody and Val had set the table with the yellow-checked cloth for the family dinner and then sat down in the living room with a jigsaw puzzle. The only sounds were the low buzz of their voices and the hum of the radio.

"It's too quiet around here," Melody said.

"I used to like the quiet," Val said, carefully fitting a piece into the puzzle. "But now I like some noise."

"Oh, that's because you're getting used to all of Big Momma's students coming and going," Melody said. She tried to press a turtle-shaped piece down. It didn't fit.

"And Poppa whistling in the morning," Val added.

Melody suddenly saw where her piece slid in perfectly. "I knew you'd like a noisy, big family as much as I do."

Val smiled shyly. "I guess I do," she said.

But the noise they heard next was unlike anything they'd ever heard before. It came from the kitchen.

"Oh, no! Oh, my goodness!" Mommy cried out.

"Lord!" Tish moaned.

Melody jumped up so quickly that she knocked the puzzle off the coffee table and broke it apart. Outside, her father was yelling, asking what was wrong. The back door opened and slammed as the men came inside.

"What do you think is going on?" Val whispered.

Melody heard her mother crying. Something terrible must have happened.

Lila came running down the stairs. "What is it?" she asked. When she saw the girls' faces, she asked again. "What?"

Mommy pushed open the kitchen door. Her eyes were red, and her face was wet with tears. Tish was right behind her, looking worried. She hurried past all of them to the phone. Daddy and Charles followed Mommy into the dining room.

Melody's stomach hurt. "Did something happen to Dwayne? Or Yvonne?"

"No, no." Mommy answered quickly. "But we heard terrible news on the radio from Alabama."

"What happened?" Lila asked.

"A church in Birmingham was bombed this morning," Mommy said.

Melody's tummy knot felt tighter. "Was it . . . was it the Russians?" she asked, confused. "Is it a war?" Mommy had said "bomb." Bombs were not by accident. At school they'd learned about countries like Russia making bombs and planning to use them against other countries, to prove they were strong.

"No, honey," Mommy said. "It's not that kind of war."

"Some people aren't happy about black people fighting for equal rights," Daddy explained. "They think bombing a church will scare us so much that we will stop marching and protesting and speaking up."

Charles looked at Tish. He was shaking his head. "This is why we left Birmingham," he said.

Tish nodded. "There have been so many bombings."

Melody couldn't understand it. She knew that people disagreed all the time, even people in the same family, like Daddy and Dwayne. But a bomb!

"What kind of people . . . I mean, how could anybody do that to a church?" Lila was still holding her open book. It was by Langston Hughes, and the title was *Laughing to Keep from Crying.*

"Did . . . did anybody . . ." Melody's throat felt tight. She couldn't get out the word that she wanted to say.

"I think lots of people must be hurt," her father said.

"Sunday school was in session," her mother whispered.

Melody walked slowly over to Mommy, who wrapped her arms around Melody. Only a few hours ago Melody had been in Sunday school herself.

Cousin Tish hung up the phone and pulled Val into a hug. "I can't get a soul on the phone," she said, her eyes wide with worry.

A car pulled into the driveway outside, and the sounds of Poppa and Big Momma filled the kitchen. "Have mercy!" Big Momma came in holding her church hat and pocketbook. "Four little girls are gone! We heard on the radio in the car."

Val burst into tears.

"Gone?" Melody asked. "You mean . . . they died? At Sunday school?" Her knees were suddenly shaky, and she sat down right on the floor, feeling as though she might throw up. She swallowed, and her tight throat hurt.

"This is insane!" Lila shouted, taking off her glasses to rub her eyes.

"It's evil." Daddy's voice shook in a way Melody had never heard before. When she looked up at him, she saw that his eyes were red, and they flashed with anger.

"How can anyone have so much hatred that they'd harm children?" Cousin Tish whispered.

Melody balled her hands into fists, determined not to cry, determined to stop her insides from shaking. She wondered how old the four girls were. She wondered if their houses would be too quiet forever, because they weren't coming home.

In the kitchen, Poppa turned from one radio station to another, but the news reports just kept saying the same thing over and over: "There's been a race bombing at the 16th Street Baptist Church in Birmingham, Alabama. The church is a meeting point for many civil rights activities.

Four Negro girls were killed in the blast, and an unknown number were injured."

Charles switched on the TV, but it was too early for the news. A sports program was on. Melody wished they would turn everything off. "Do we have to listen?" she asked.

"No, child, we don't," Big Momma said gently. She began to sing. Her voice was a contralto. It was rich and deep and, now, sad.

> *There is a balm in Gilead,*
> *to make the wounded whole.*
> *There is a balm in Gilead,*
> *to heal the sin-sick soul.*

Melody knew the song. It was about healing. She closed her eyes, and then blinked them open, breathing hard. But she didn't sing.

No Words

Melody went home with her sister and parents in silence. Her head was spinning. Her stomach was spinning. Her throat felt as if it was throbbing open and closed. She had no more questions or words.

Lila went straight to the TV. "Oh, Daddy!" she called. "They're showing pictures of that church!"

Mommy went upstairs, and Daddy stood with Lila in front of the television. Melody didn't want to look. The telephone rang, and she hurried to answer it.

"Hello?" Melody sounded like she had a cold.

"Hello? Hello?" It was Dwayne!

Melody tried to clear her throat. "Dwayne! Are you . . . are you okay?"

"Yeah, yeah. We just played at Clark College in Atlanta last night, and they put us up in the dorms. Man, the kids here are out of their minds over what happened in Birmingham. I can't believe it—a church on Sunday morning! That's some crazy, scary stuff. Listen, I just called to let Mom and Dad know I'm all right. My pay-phone money is gonna run out. Let me speak to Mom."

"Mommy, Dwayne is—" Melody tried to shout, but her voice was scratchy and faint.

"I've got it, Melody," Mommy called down. There was a click, and Mommy picked up the upstairs phone.

Melody hung up, relieved that her brother was all right. Then she ran upstairs and curled up on her bed, staring at the poster from the Walk to Freedom. She stayed that way for a long time—long enough to hear the water running as Lila brushed her teeth and Lila's bed squeaking when she lay down on it. Long enough to hear her parents murmuring to each other after Daddy came slowly up the stairs.

Melody tried to sleep, but sleep wouldn't come. *What were those little girls doing when the explosion happened? Laughing? Praying? Singing? What were their names?* Finally Melody closed her eyes, and when she opened them it was daylight again. Monday morning. Melody blinked at the Mickey Mouse clock.

"You okay?" Lila asked softly. "You tossed and turned all night."

Melody opened her mouth to speak, but a strange croaking sound came out.

Lila stopped buttoning her blouse. "What's the matter with you?"

Melody tried to answer, but croaked again. She put a hand to her throat.

"I'm going to get Mommy," Lila said, rushing out of the room. She came back with their mother, who was half dressed for work.

"What is it, baby? What is it?"

Melody shook her head, trying to say something.

"With all that singing you've been doing, you may have laryngitis," Mommy said, smoothing Melody's hair. "I want you to stay home from rehearsal tonight."

Melody opened her mouth to protest, but Mommy put her finger to Melody's lips. "No school today, either. You'll stay with Big Momma. She'll take good care of you."

The next thing Melody knew, she was riding to her grandparents' house, still in her pajamas. Val met them at the door. Mommy and Big Momma whispered in the kitchen before Mommy came to kiss Melody on the forehead and slip out.

"What happened?" Val looked worried. "Mama said you can't go to school today."

"My throat," Melody whispered. She really wanted to talk to Val about yesterday. Was she still upset, too? Had she been able to sleep last night? But Melody didn't get a chance. Tish came out of the kitchen wearing her salon smock.

"Let's go, baby," Tish said to Val. "I have an early customer."

Val slung her book bag over her shoulder. "Mama is driving me to school," she told Melody. "She says she doesn't want me walking for a while. She'll give you a ride, too, tomorrow."

Melody nodded as Val and her mother left. Then the house was totally quiet.

Big Momma had put soft pillows on the sofa in the living room. "Have a little of this," she said, placing a mug of lemony-smelling tea on a flower-shaped coaster at one end of the coffee table.

Melody sipped some and then eased back onto the pillows. Her throat hurt a little when the sweet liquid trickled down.

"You just rest," Big Momma said. "I'm canceling my lessons for today, so you can stay right here." Big Momma went upstairs, and Melody could hear her speaking in low tones on the phone.

Melody tried to get comfortable. She rolled onto her side, facing the piano. The heavy old upright was as tall as Melody was, with flowers carved into its music stand. The keys were no longer black and white, but had aged to a worn blackish-brown and tan. But Big Momma kept it tuned so that it played like it was new. Melody wondered if human voices could be tuned when they became worn.

Lift every voice and sing. She mouthed the words silently

as she lay back on the sofa. Melody couldn't go on, even in her mind. What if she couldn't sing again? Youth Day was only a few weeks away. They were supposed to practice twice a week until then. She had to get better.

♫

Charles stopped by during his lunch hour to bring Melody some special drops from the pharmacy for her throat.

"You just suck on these like candy," he said. "They'll melt in your mouth. Don't talk any more than you have to." Melody was glad she didn't have to say anything. She popped one of the rosy-colored lozenges into her mouth. It was warm and soothing and tasted like cherry.

For lunch, Big Momma gave Melody soup and brought her a brand-new book of paper dolls that she'd been saving for a birthday. Melody ate the soup but couldn't concentrate on cutting out the paper dolls neatly. She rolled another cherry drop around in her mouth as her thoughts kept going back to Birmingham.

What did the four little girls look like? Were they dark brown, with skinny legs, and did they run so fast that their hair came undone? Were they tall and golden, with ponytails that bounced and swung from side to side when they talked and waved their hands? Did they have sisters and brothers? The thought that something awful like this could happen to Melody's brother or sisters—or her cousin Val—shook her.

Melody heard Val come in the front door. It seemed like she was home much earlier than usual.

"Melody! Can you talk yet?" Val dropped her book bag with a thump near the TV.

Melody discovered that she could whisper. "How'd you get here so fast?"

"Sharon's mother picked us up. I got your homework. School was so weird today! Nobody knew the girls in Alabama, but we were sad like we did."

Melody nodded and sat up straight. Suddenly she wanted to do something that would take her mind off all the sadness. "Let's go out," she whispered.

Val made a face. "In your pajamas? You'd better put on some of my clothes." Melody smiled and realized that she hadn't smiled at all since yesterday. She borrowed a pair of Val's shorts and a shirt.

"What do you want to do outside?" Val asked, changing out of her school clothes.

"Plant," Melody whispered. Poppa had bought dozens of tulip and daffodil bulbs from the Eastern Market downtown over the summer. He and Melody had planned to plant them before the frost. She knew that in spring the bulbs would push through the ground and bloom—the first flowers of the season. Poppa always reminded her that every season brought change.

In the yard, Melody felt like a mime she'd seen on TV. She used her hands to go through the motions, showing Val what to do.

"I got it!" Val said, digging with her spade just the way Melody did.

Melody wished she could use her voice to explain that thinking of new flowers blooming made her feel that the world didn't have to be ugly and bad, but could also be good and beautiful.

Val held up one of the dusty brown bulbs to look at it closely. "It's hard to believe these things will grow into something pretty someday," she said.

Melody only nodded. She couldn't help thinking again of the girls who wouldn't grow up at all.

♫

By Thursday, Melody's speaking voice was almost back to normal. Mommy had kept her home from school all week, so Melody had to beg her to let her go to choir practice.

"Do you think you will be able to sing?" Mommy asked in the car after supper.

"I hope so," Melody said.

Mommy drove up in front of the church. "You girls go on in. I'm going to find a spot to park and meet you inside."

Val and Lila got out. As Melody followed, Mommy asked her if she'd brought the throat lozenges from Charles.

"Yes, but I don't think I'll need them," Melody said. Mommy seemed satisfied. Melody got out of the car and started toward the wide stone steps leading up to the open doors.

The adult choir was clapping and singing, *"Oh, freedom! Oh, freedom! Oh, freedom over me."*

Melody's steps slowed, and her heart beat faster. The voices were familiar. The song was familiar. Yet somehow each beat and each step went through her entire body. *Thump, thump.* She heard her own heartbeat loudly in her ears. At the top step she stopped.

Val's face popped around the door frame. "What's taking you so long?"

Melody couldn't answer, because she did not know.

The adults were finished by the time Melody got inside. Miss Dorothy came up behind her. "I'm glad you're here, Melody, but don't feel that you have to sing tonight."

Melody was mystified by the way she was feeling. Every one of her footsteps seemed to tingle. Her throat began to throb. Miss Dorothy was still talking, but she sounded farther and farther away.

"Melody?" Someone was calling her name. It was Mommy.

Melody blinked. Faces were crowded around her. She froze right in the middle of the center aisle.

"Melody!" Mommy shook her. Melody opened her mouth to answer. Nothing came out. Not a whisper, not a croak. Nothing. Suddenly Melody just had to get out. She wanted to be anywhere other than a church! She jerked away from her mother and ran for the door.

"Dee-Dee!" Lila shouted.

"Melody!" Val called. "Come back!"

Melody ran outside, down the steps, and straight into Big Momma.

"Melody! What is it?"

"She's lost her voice again!" Lila called.

Big Momma took Melody's hand and started up the steps, but Melody shook her head hard, pulling away.

Her grandmother took one look at her and then called out to Lila. "You go on back inside," she said. "Tell your mother that I'm taking Melody home."

Big Momma raised Melody's chin with one of her strong hands and looked deep into her eyes. Melody burst into tears.

"It's not only your throat that's hurting, is it? Something

more is wrong," Big Momma said. "It's your heart that's hurting for those four little girls in Birmingham."

Melody nodded, still breathing hard, still feeling her heartbeats thumping.

"And you don't feel very good about going into the church right now."

Melody nodded again.

"I know. Honey, don't be afraid of the building. This is God's house. Everyone here loves you." Big Momma wrapped her arms around Melody. "Baby chick, I know it's hard to understand. Life is so special, so precious—and anyone who would take a life just doesn't hold love in his heart. There's no understanding it, but we have to stand up to the wrong of it. We have to keep our hearts and voices strong in the face of such a wrong."

Melody swallowed hard. How could she ever be strong, when she felt so bad?

Whispers

Big Momma told only Mommy and Daddy that Melody was afraid of being in church. Melody was embarrassed for anyone else to know, even Val. The idea that she might ruin Youth Day troubled Melody more than losing her voice did.

Instead of sending her to school on Friday, Mommy took Melody to the doctor. He looked into Melody's ears and looked down her throat and listened to her chest.

"I don't see anything that's really wrong," the doctor said. "There's no swelling in her throat. You say she's been rehearsing for a big singing performance?"

"Yes," Mommy said. She looked at Melody but didn't say anything else to the doctor.

"She's not sick," the doctor insisted. He scratched his head. "Maybe it's stage fright," he said.

Melody looked at her mother. He was getting close to the truth without giving her any way to fix things. She wanted to leave.

"She's been singing in front of audiences since she was three," Mommy said.

"Well, then," the doctor said. "We'll just have to wait for her voice to come back on its own."

Melody pointed at a pad on the examining room counter. The doctor handed it to her with a pen.

What if it doesn't come back? she wrote.

"Oh, it will," the doctor said. "Sooner or later."

"Is there anything we can do?" Mommy asked.

"I suggest warm drinks and whatever else soothes her throat."

Melody hung her head. She'd been drinking tea and hot lemonade till she thought she might float away. She'd swallowed spoonfuls of honey, as Miss Dorothy suggested. She'd sucked so many of Charles's lozenges that she wasn't sure she liked cherry-flavored anything anymore.

The doctor peered over his glasses at Melody. "This must be a very special performance," he said. "Or a mighty special song."

Yes! Melody wanted to say. *I want to lift my voice and sing, but I can't! Now I'm letting everybody down.*

"Thank you, doctor," Mommy said as Melody hopped down from the table.

Mommy tried to cheer up Melody in the car by telling her they'd have a big pancake breakfast on Sunday morning. Melody knew that was because they wouldn't be going to church.

Melody looked out the passenger window at the Detroit streets, where people were walking and talking and living their lives. A memory flashed in her mind of the TV screen and a quick glimpse of smoking bricks. Nobody would be going to the 16th Street Baptist Church in Birmingham on Sunday. Melody shivered.

Would she ever be able to *not* remember?

Melody was surprised that Daddy was home from work when they got there. He smelled like cinnamon when he gave her a hug.

"What did the doctor say?" Daddy asked.

"Wait for her voice to come back. Warm liquids," Mommy said.

Daddy smiled. "Well, how did I know that? I've got my all-time special Daddy cocoa with cinnamon sticks and whipped cream ready!"

Daddy only made cocoa when snow had fallen outside and everyone except Mommy had been out shoveling. Melody followed him to the kitchen. There was her favorite mug on the counter, waiting to be filled.

"You sit right there," Daddy said, tilting his head toward Melody's seat at the table. He poured the steaming cocoa into her mug without any spills and added the whipped cream just as there was a knock on the back door. In came Poppa and Val.

Poppa was carrying a small basket of pink carnations with sprigs of eucalyptus tucked at the edges. "How's our girl?" he asked, kissing the top of Melody's head.

Melody was beginning to feel uncomfortable with all the attention. She wasn't really sick. But she didn't feel well either. Her voice was refusing to work. And despite what Big Momma had told her, she just wasn't sure that their church was safe. Couldn't hateful people choose any church to blow up?

Val held something that looked like a folded sheet of construction paper. "Sharon asked me to give this to you. Your class made you a get-well card," she explained as she sat down.

Melody pushed her mug of cocoa aside and opened the card. There were the names of everybody in her class, including her teacher. Big block letters said "GET WELL SOON." Next to Sharon's and Diane's names were drawings of small musical notes. Val had signed her name in one corner.

"I know I'm not in the same class as you, but I wanted to sign it, too," she said.

Melody mouthed the words "Thank you." She was feeling very tired. Not being able to talk was hard. Trying not to feel was harder.

"We're going to go," Poppa said, nodding to Val.

Val didn't seem to want to leave, but she got up anyway. "I'll come by tomorrow," she said.

When they were gone, Daddy picked Melody up, the same way he used to when she was tiny, and carried her to bed. "You have a big heart for such a little person," he whispered to her. "You take your time finding your way."

Melody wasn't sure what Daddy meant, but she rested her head on his shoulder, calmed by the steady beat of his heart.

♫

Everyone tried to help Melody get her voice back and get her spirits up. On Saturday morning, she woke to hear the phone ringing. Lila was already up and out. Mickey Mouse was pointing to ten. Melody couldn't believe she'd slept so late.

"Melody! Telephone, in my room!" Mommy called. Melody frowned as she got up. Mommy knew she couldn't speak. Why would she make her come to the phone?

Mommy patted their blue-striped bedspread, handed Melody the telephone, and then slipped out of the room. Melody sat on the edge of the bed and held the receiver up to her ear.

"Dee-Dee, this is Vonnie. I know you can't talk. Just listen. I want you to know that the bombing in Birmingham won't stop us. Remember that lady who was afraid to vote? We went back this week, and she signed up. We've been singing 'Ain't Gonna Let Nobody Turn Me Around.' You know that one. Don't let anything turn *you* around. You've been working so hard on this song. The New Hope choir needs you. Don't be afraid to let your Dee-Dee light shine and shine and shine, you hear?"

Melody wanted so much to tell Yvonne that she *did* hear.

"Tap on the receiver if you get what I'm saying."

Melody tapped three times.

"Good!" Yvonne said. "I wish I could be there to hear you. You can do it! Love you. Bye!"

Melody sat for a minute after she hung up the phone. She was happy that her big sister hadn't forgotten her. If Yvonne believed in her, maybe she *could* go back to the church.

♪

On Monday morning, Melody still couldn't talk, but she went back to school. She felt as if she'd been away for more than a week. Everything seemed so different.

When they got home that afternoon, Lila opened the mailbox. "You got mail," she said, handing Melody a long plain envelope.

Melody didn't recognize the return address, but she

knew the scratchy, cramped handwriting. She took the
letter to her room and stretched across her bed to read it.

Dear Melody,

*I bet you're shocked that your brother can write a whole
page! Are you jazzed about taking over Youth Day? I heard
you were having throat problems, but I'm sure that's all over
now and you can't wait to sing your solo.*

*I am learning a whole lot about the music business. On
the road, we're just colored people, like anybody else. Not
even the big names can stay in the white hotels. Can you dig
that? I mean, these guys have sold thousands of records, but
they have to go in the back doors to perform in the top clubs!
At the colleges, it's all right. But I thought talent would get
more respect. Seems like our talent is colored first, and great
second. I'm not quitting, though. I love seeing how the crowds
enjoy my voice. I can't wait until I'm singing my own songs!
I'm not letting any stupid laws or crazy ideas about us hold
me back. I know I'm good! You're good, too . . . almost as good
as me. Ha, ha! Best of luck on your big day.*

Your one and only brother-man,
Dwayne

Melody rolled over on her back and read the letter
again. Dwayne had been so sure that fairness would come

along with fame! It sounded like it hadn't. At least not yet. She folded the letter carefully and slipped it under her pillow. Melody remembered her father saying something about the men he knew who had given up when the music business got hard. But Dwayne wasn't giving up. She decided she wouldn't give up either.

Melody turned on the tape recorder to listen to her song again. She pictured Dwayne in front of the college crowds. When she opened her mouth to sing, the words came out!

Melody jumped up. She started the tape over, and she sang the entire first verse. Her voice was a bit squeaky, but she wasn't whispering.

"Dee-Dee!" Lila stepped in from the hall. "You're singing again! This means you can practice! This means Youth Day might not be a disaster! I'm going to tell Mommy."

"No." Melody took a deep breath. "I will."

Voices Lifted

elody called Val and then Sharon. She even called Diane. They were all thrilled to hear Melody's voice.

"Can you really sing?" Sharon asked when Mommy dropped Melody, Val, and Lila in front of the church for choir practice that night.

"I think so," Melody said. She was starting to feel nervous again.

"Well, let's find out," Sharon said, waving them toward the church.

At the steps, Melody froze. She couldn't make herself move. Her insides shook, and the awful fear came back.

"I . . . I can't!" She looked at Val.

"Maybe if you just take one step at a time," Val suggested, taking Melody's hand.

"No. Don't make me." Melody pulled her hand away from her cousin's.

"I'll get Miss Dorothy," Lila said, sprinting up the steps.

Melody didn't care who they got—she could not, would not go in. If she did, she might be silenced again.

"What is it, exactly?" Sharon whispered.

Melody wasn't sure what her friends would say if she told them the truth. She swallowed, half expecting her throat to close up again.

Mommy came around the corner from the parking lot at the same time Miss Dorothy came out of the church. They both hurried to where Melody stood at the bottom of the steps.

"Melody, I'm happy you've recovered your voice," Miss Dorothy said. "However . . ."

Melody sighed. "I know. If I can't come into the church, I can't do the solo."

Miss Dorothy looked sad. "If you can't, the choir will have to perform a song it already knows. And," she added, "I will have to choose a different soloist."

"We understand," her mother said. "Don't we, Melody?"

"Yes, Mommy."

Melody sat in the car while Lila and Val went into the church to rehearse. Melody needed time to think. She had to figure out what to do. Months ago, when Miss Dorothy had asked her to perform a solo, she had been so proud! When she had finally picked her song, she had wanted to understand what the lyrics were trying to tell the world.

Then the church in Birmingham was bombed, and those girls died. Her voice had died with them, and now she was afraid of a place that had meant so much to her.

Melody remembered Yvonne's words: *Don't let anything turn you around.* When rehearsal was over and everyone got into the car, Melody leaned over and whispered into her cousin's ear, "I need help."

♪

After school the next day, Val, Sharon, and Diane sat with Melody around Big Momma's kitchen table. "I can't go into the church because I'm scared," Melody said. "I can't figure out how not to be."

"But what are you scared of in our church?" Sharon asked.

Diane was frowning. "It's not anything in our church," she said, looking steadily at Melody. "It's what happened to the girls in the church in Birmingham, right?"

"Right," Melody said. There, it was out.

"That scared *everybody*, Melody. Even grown-ups," Val said.

"I still have bad dreams about it," Sharon admitted.

"You do?" Melody was surprised. She had thought she was the only one who was having bad dreams.

Sharon nodded. "We talked about it at school."

"Last week," Diane nodded. "But you weren't there."

"I didn't know that," Melody said.

"I know you worked hard on that song," Diane said. "We won't let you down, and you can't let us down."

Melody tugged at one of her braids. "But what if I lose

my voice again? What if I think about the Birmingham girls and—"

"We'll all go inside together," Sharon said. "You don't have to be scared."

"*We're* four little girls," Val pointed out.

Melody nodded. She felt stronger now that she wasn't hiding her fear. Maybe she could do this for the four girls who would never speak again. Maybe she could lift her voice and sing, just for them.

♫

On the first Saturday of October, Melody stood in the midst of the excited young people gathering outside New Hope Baptist Church. Buses were pulled up to the curb, and cars were dropping people off. There were children from choirs all over Detroit.

"I'm nervous," Melody sighed. Their plan had worked for the last three practices. All the girls had met out front and walked into the church together. Today, that seemed impossible. The steps were crowded, and groups of people blocked the front doors.

Melody took a deep breath. "Can we just go in?"

The girls clasped each other's hands tightly and spread out side by side on one step.

"Ready?" Sharon asked.

"Ready!" the others practically shouted, and they all

started to march up the church steps. Halfway up, two older ladies cut into the group, separating Melody and Diane from the others. Melody felt her hand dangle free, but she kept going. In the vestibule, Melody and Diane were separated by the crowd. Melody was alone.

Melody stood at the edge of the center aisle. Her heart fluttered. People were surging around her. It was no use trying to find the other girls again—she had to get to the choir. Melody started walking. The organist was playing softly, and the sound echoed all around Melody.

I have to do this, she told herself. *For the girls who can't go to church.* Melody saw Miss Dorothy at the front of the room. They locked eyes, and Melody kept stepping. When Melody was halfway up the aisle, Val appeared from somewhere and grabbed her hand. Then Sharon appeared and took Melody's other hand.

When they made it to the front, Melody was trembling. She took her seat in the first row. Diane rushed up, breathless. After Pastor Daniels welcomed everyone, Miss Dorothy stood with her baton. The choir rose and took their places at the front of the church.

Melody stepped forward as the introduction began. In a move she did not expect, her three friends stepped forward, too. Melody wanted to say something to thank them, but she couldn't. It was her time to sing.

Val appeared from somewhere and grabbed her hand.
Then Sharon appeared and took Melody's other hand.

Lift every voice and sing,
Till earth and heaven ring,
Ring with the harmonies of liberty;
Let our rejoicing rise,
High as the list'ning skies,
Let it resound loud as the rolling sea.

The chorus joined in, and it sounded as if Miss Dorothy's piano and their voices were doing a kind of dance.

Sing a song full of the faith
that the dark past has taught us,
Sing a song full of the hope
that the present has brought us;
Facing the rising sun of our new day begun,
Let us march on till victory is won.

The four girls held tightly to each other's hands. The audience clapped, and cheered, and stomped. It was no ordinary sound. Melody was overwhelmed by it, and also by the truth of the words they'd just sung. She scanned the packed room for her parents, or for Val's parents, but she couldn't find them. Then she looked to the place where Big Momma had been sitting, but she wasn't there.

Dwayne was. He was wearing a black suit and a purple

shirt and tie. He was clapping and cheering.

Melody felt faith and hope and rejoicing all at once.

When there was a break in the program, Melody rushed out into the congregation and threw her arms around her brother. "Dwayne!" she cried. "You came!"

"I wouldn't miss it. You were fantastic!"

Melody stood back to look into his eyes. "Really?"

Dwayne nodded and draped an arm around her shoulders. "No kidding, kid. I knew nothing could keep you quiet for long. I just want to ask you, now that you're famous and everything—"

"Dwayne!"

"You think you might find time to do some backup singing when I cut my first record in a few months?"

Melody stared at him, wide-eyed. "You mean it?"

"Of course! But let's keep it between you and me for now." Dwayne craned his neck as he searched the crowd for the rest of the family. "I see Big Momma," he said, taking Melody's hand. "Let's go."

Melody felt herself grinning as she followed her brother. She had regained her voice, and it had been the hardest, scariest experience she'd ever had. Now she knew she would never stop speaking out for what was right. Melody Ellison would never, ever stop singing.

Inside
Melody's World

The 1960s were an important decade for the civil rights movement in America—and Melody's hometown of Detroit was an important city. Thousands of African Americans worked in Detroit's car factories, just like Melody's father. Detroit was also home to some of the country's first African American theater companies, radio stations, publishing houses, and history museums.

When Melody's story takes place, Detroit had more independent black-owned businesses than any other

Greetings from
Detroit
MICHIGAN
"The MOTOR CAPITAL of the WORLD"

Above: A postcard shows many of Detroit's landmarks, including skyscrapers and a bridge to Canada. Right: the Ford car factory.

city in the United States. The most well known was Motown Records, fondly called "Hitsville, U.S.A." The "Motown Sound" quickly became famous and influenced music all over the world. People of all races listened to and loved the music that was born in

The name "Motown" is a tribute to Detroit, which is known as "The Motor City." Today, the Motown studio is a museum.

Detroit. Some famous Motown artists include Diana Ross and The Supremes, Smokey Robinson, and many others.

While many African Americans had good lives in Detroit, they still experienced segregation and discrimination. There were no "Whites Only" signs on businesses in Detroit, but African Americans could be refused service in stores, restaurants, and even hospitals. Black children went to separate schools, which often had fewer supplies than schools for white children. Some black people were not allowed to buy or rent homes

The Supremes perform in Detroit.

White homeowners in Detroit protested a housing project for black families in 1942.

in neighborhoods that were mostly white. This sort of discrimination existed all across America.

Throughout the country, people spoke up about and fought for equal rights for black people. Activism was an important part of Detroit's culture. The city had the largest chapter of the National Association for the Advancement of Colored People, or NAACP, and children as young as Melody were involved in the youth council. Detroit hosted the Walk to Freedom to support civil rights struggles in the South and to call attention to the inequalities that existed

The sign on the bus celebrates Detroit's NAACP youth council as "the largest branch in the USA."

Marchers filled the streets of Detroit for the Walk to Freedom (left) and gathered in front of the Lincoln Memorial in the nation's capital for the March on Washington (below).

in the North. With a crowd of more than 125,000 people, it was the largest civil rights demonstration in America up to that point. Dr. Martin Luther King Jr. attended the event and first gave his now-famous "I Have a Dream" speech.

Dr. King delivered a version of that same speech two months later at the March on Washington, where more than 250,000 people gathered. People all over the world watched the historic event on television.

Many felt hopeful that equality for everyone was possible.

But less than three weeks later, an African American church was bombed in Birmingham, Alabama. The racially motivated hate crime killed four innocent girls. The tragedy left the world in shock and a nation in mourning. In her story, Melody was afraid to go to her own church afterward, for fear she would be in danger, too.

It took strength and courage for people to continue

Today, a statue across from the 16th Street Baptist Church in Birmingham honors the four young girls who were killed in the 1963 bombing.

Students in Birmingham in 1963, marching through the streets of their city singing feedom songs.

fighting for civil rights. Several key leaders kept the movment going, but hundreds of thousands of ordinary citizens also played a role, however small. Children like Melody made a difference. They attended marches, participated in boycotts, and even spent time in jail. They lifted their voices in protest of inequality and in praise of social justice.

♪ A Sneak Peek at ♪

Never Stop Singing

It's 1964, and Melody has just turned ten! She comes up with an idea to make her community better but discovers that being a leader isn't easy.

t eleven-thirty on December 31, Melody walked into New Hope Baptist Church and settled into her seat between Lila and Yvonne. She had sat between her sisters ever since she was a tiny girl. Now, half an hour away from turning ten, Melody felt very grown-up.

Pastor Daniels stepped up to the pulpit. "Good evening!" the preacher said. His voice was always loud and clear, and he never needed to use a microphone.

"Good evening!" everyone answered together.

Pastor Daniels peered out at the crowd over the tops of his glasses. "A week ago, many of us received gifts," he began. "Isn't that right?"

"Yes, sir!" a young voice answered from the back. A few people laughed, and Melody turned to look.

Pastor Daniels chuckled. "Well, New Hope church family, at midnight everyone here will receive another gift. When the New Year comes in, each of us will receive a new opportunity to make a difference in the world. And I want each one of you to ask yourself: What will *I* do to help justice, equality, and dignity grow in our community?"

Melody sat up a little straighter. She thought of the seeds she and Poppa planted in their gardens every spring and of the work it took to make those seeds grow and blossom. *Can a person really make justice, equality, and dignity grow, too?* she wondered. *How?*

Pastor Daniels kept speaking. "In honor of all those hopeful souls who first sat watch for their freedom so long ago, now is the time for every one of us to use this gift we receive tonight. I want each of you to pick one thing you can work on, just one thing you can change for the better, right here in our community."

Murmurs rippled through the congregation.

"I want you to give this idea some serious thought," Pastor Daniels said. "But don't take too long. When Reverend Dr. King visited with us here in Detroit last summer, he said, '*Now* is the time to lift our nation.' Now is the time, New Hope, for us to lift *our* nation. Now is the time for you"—he pointed one way— "and you"—he pointed the other way—"and you! To take action!"

Melody was sure he was looking directly at her. She held her breath.

"The new year, 1964, is a season of change. Change yourself. Change our community. Change our nation!"

a Nez Perce girl who loves daring
adventures on horseback

a Jewish girl with a secret
ambition to be an actress

who joins the war effort
when Hawaii is attacked

whose big ideas get her into
trouble—but also save the day

who finds the strength to lift
her voice for those who can't

who fights for the right to play
on the boys' basketball team